INSIGHT IS BETTER THAN ICE CREAM

Insight is Better Than Ice Cream

by Frank Crocitto

Candlepower Communications
New York

For information contact:
Discovery Institute
64 Plains Road
New Paltz, New York 12561
914 255-5548 discover@bestweb.net

Author: Frank Crocitto
Editor: Jeremiah Horrigan
Jacket Design: David Perry
Book Design: Patricia Kane Horrigan
Original Art: Grady Kane-Horrigan

ISBN: 0-9677558-0-8
First Edition

For my grandmother…

AN INVITATION
TO FRANK CROCITTO'S *INSIGHT*
BY HIS FRIEND,
JEREMIAH HORRIGAN

This book is dedicated to the memory of Diana Casamassima Tarulli, a cheerfully persistent Italian grandmother who never stopped trying to put some meat on the bones of her skinny grandson.

When young Frankie balked at eating some bitter-tasting thing that was, of course, good for him — boiled broccoli rabe, for example — his grandmother would coax him:

"Eat, Frangeesk, *mange*," she'd urge in her thick Barese accent. "Just taste it, try it, Frankie. It's better than ice cream."

Frankie knew, as all boys know, that nothing in the world is better than ice cream. He knew this as surely as he knew that the hometown

Brooklyn Dodgers were Destiny's Darlings, or that a hot summer's day was a foretaste of Paradise. So what was his grandmother saying? Was this revolting green stuff better than a *Creamsicle*?

His senses told him to stay away. But he heard the wisdom behind his grandmother's words. He would do what she asked. He would try it.

It tasted far worse than he expected. That first bite was bitter beyond words. Worse than spinach. He swallowed, then stuffed his mouth with bread to kill the taste. His grandmother smiled. She never gave up.

The urgings continued, meal after meal. More tastings, more bread. More patient smiles.

Gradually, almost without his knowing it, something changed. It wasn't that the bitterness had disappeared. There was something besides or perhaps within the bitterness, some unexpected, un-guessed-at taste that took him by slow surprise. The broccoli rabe had a strange, deep down flavor. It was certainly not sweet, but it had a somehow enlivening quality that quietly conquered Frankie's ideas and worries, until, in the end, ice cream came to seem a laughably cheap and chilly thrill.

But, since you can no more judge a book by its title than by its cover, let me tell you about the book's and its author's histories.

The teaching tales in this volume originally appeared in *Chronogram*, a monthly magazine published in New Paltz, N.Y. (By no coincidence at all, New Paltz is also the home of Discovery Institute, a school of practical wisdom established in 1980 by Frank.)

Each "Frankly Speaking" column was usually a pointed reminiscence on the magazine's monthly themes (i.e., religion, sex, cars, etc.). We've arranged these stories in rough chronological order. The earliest selections are set against the bustling panorama of an Italian-American boyhood in Brooklyn. Later come stories of his college days, his adventures in Off-Broadway bohemia and finally stories set in the greener pastures of upstate New York.

During Frank's bohemian days, about half way through his 62 years, when he was a rising star in theatrical circles, he discovered something that turned his life around. He found it quite accidentally, as you'll read in "Affidavit of an Outsider." He heard a radio broadcast, which led him to a book, which in turn took him to a school. He entered that School of Practical Philosophy as a student and then began a period of learning that culminated in his becoming a teacher of what is known (to those who have discovered it) as the Work.

This string of discoveries saved Frank's life, though it did little to change its outward appearance or fatten his wallet. He studied and worked on himself at the school for 13 years while continuing his life in the theater and later as a teacher, a journalist and even a milkman. That's one of the grand things about the Work — there's no running off to monasteries or weaving hair shirts. Your ordinary, problem-plagued life is the perfect place for you to start working on yourself. And so it was for Frank.

I mentioned that Frank was a teacher. If you ask old pals like Vince or Louie or Paulie, guys from his old neighborhood, they'll tell you that's one thing about Frank that's never really changed. Yeah, he was fast on his feet, a good stickball pitcher, so-so scholar, what they call in Brooklyn "a regulah guy." But other guys fit that description. What set Frank apart was that he was always a teacher. Teaching was something he was always doing. Here's how he describes it in the story "Me and Michelangelo":

"I used to teach on the street corners of Brooklyn, year round, even in the bitter cold when we'd huddle around the shoulders of a building, stamping our feet and rubbing our hands together just to keep warm. I just did it. I had the gift ... We all do what we can't help doing."

He went so far as to teach professionally in the factory-like public and private education system. But when he discovered the School of Practical Philosophy, he found a teaching that recognized and combatted the suffocating mechanicalness of everyday life. It gave him the focus and knowledge and practice he had hungered for since his earliest days. (Check out "A Rope Thrown From Above.")

The Work that ignited Frank's life provides an eminently practical approach to life's great questions. Brought to the West by George Gurdjieff, it draws upon all the great spiritual traditions to present its students with a way of recognizing and ultimately overcoming the mechanicality of ordinary life.

Simply put, the Work says that most of us, most of the time, are asleep. Asleep to reality, asleep to our potential as human beings, asleep to our true natures. Nature has taken *homo sapiens* as far as she can; the next step in man's evolution is man's to take. The teaching provides the knowledge needed for men and women, studying and working under the guidance of a teacher within the discipline of a school setting, to take that next step.

So what has all that got to do with the price of apples? Or the taste of broccoli rabe?

The idea is this: in order to gain anything worth gaining, to take a step toward knowing, you have to be willing to have an experience, no matter how bitter you expect it to be.

The world as we know it, the world of sleep and mechanicalness, offers us ice cream, sweet and seductive, but cold and lifeless. The teaching says there are other, more nourishing foods to be found, sometimes in the most unlikely places. All that's required is a willingness to entertain the possibility of change, to let go of the convictions and opinions that keep us locked in place, that prevent us from looking for the deeper, truer sweetness of things.

What Frank found in his grandmother's

kitchen was very much like what he found in the Work — the best way to test an assertion is to put away your prejudices and taste what happens. Neither believe nor disbelieve. Don't take anything on faith, just take it and see what comes. Maybe it works for you, maybe it doesn't. Maybe you find your way to something truer and maybe you don't.

At least this way — the Work Way — you don't have to take grandma's word for what you're missing.

Contents

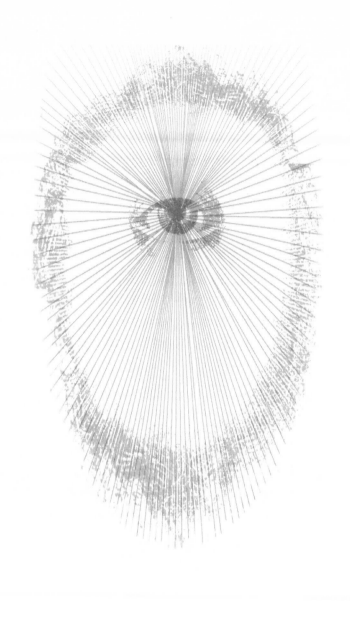

A Life Within A Life

The disadvantage I find with being a teacher is that people want to know what I teach. This used to be easy to answer when I taught English and Math and History and Music and Art and Gymnastics and Flute-Making.

Now, depending upon what I think the questioner will understand, I give all kinds of answers:

I teach the Truth.

I teach how to become yourself.

I teach a practical method of self-discovery.

I teach the development of attention.

I teach the way to develop your potential.

I teach the way to live a real life.

I teach common sense.

I teach divine common sense.

I teach self-transformation.

I teach what you already know, but have forgotten.

I teach the technique of self-creation.

On and on. Usually the questioner smiles, nods appreciatively and changes the subject.

So, finding this unsatisfactory, I keep looking for a way to characterize what I teach that is honest, accurate and doesn't cause an interested person to shut down.

And I think I've found it. I can give the answer in the form of a story.

A couple of weeks ago I went to the airport. On the way I was ruminating on that piece of popular advice: "Get a Life!" It has a nice ring to it. Most of us have heard it aimed at us, or else we've aimed it at others. And since there's always a new breeze of wisdom blowing through, it tends to echo in many a mouth.

But what it really means isn't definite. Get a new job? A new relationship? Get another attitude, a new lifestyle, what? It's one of those catch phrases that can mean most anything. And, of all the things it might mean, perhaps there's something profound to be found in it.

So I'm standing in line at the airport when I hear some voices ahead of me tangled in a loud, intense conversation. The loudest voice belonged to a large man in a dark blue coat who was leaving last-minute orders with a little blond lady who could have been his wife, or his personal slave, and a younger man, an eager man wearing a gray and fading face. Apparently, the large man was leaving the care of his most important affairs in the hands of two past masters of ineptitude. Every subject was gone over again and again; every last detail had to be nailed down.

There was talk of stocks and bonds, of a garage door that had to be locked, a timer on the living room light to be set, a package to be Fed-

Ex'd, cider that had gone bad, a sack of potatoes in the cellar, phone calls to be returned, a person in Cleveland not to be called ever again, a pair of shoes at the shoemaker's, overdue library books and a particular dentist who with all his family and close friends needed to be shot.

The man in blue was leaving for a week, though it sounded as if he were wrapping up a lifetime. There were moments in his cannonading when he reached such towering heights I doubted he could ever pull himself away and go down the boarding ramp. He was an immense man with great rolling eyes, and he lurched to and from his place in line as each new urgency swept into his mind. His little blond wife (with sequins on her bird's-nest hat) could not get anything right, and the eager young man couldn't take notes fast enough.

Here was a man, I thought, who needed to get a life, although from his perspective he already had one and was really living it. He was going places. He was getting things done. He was a man of affairs.

The man was a victim of his own life. He was being eaten up by it. All of him, all of his interest and attention was being swallowed whole by this so-called life of his. The *sturm und drang* of it so held him in thrall that he was oblivious to everything else. He was spinning. The circumstances of his life occupied and preoccupied him. He had no inner sense of his existence. He couldn't see himself, didn't know himself — he didn't even know he had a self to know. He was a hollow man caught up in a life that was fast unraveling.

Then I realized that this large, loud-mouthed man in the blue coat was not an isolated phenomenon. All of us are in that same predicament until we "get a life."

Like him, we have a semblance of a life; a life of running and jogging, of getting and spending, of planning and worrying. It's a seeming life. All our accomplishments, the checklist of errands done day after day, the phone calls made, the miles earned, the houses bought, the houses sold, the money made, the money spent, the marriage, the divorce, the settlement, the children's college, the loan gotten, the deals cut, the medical check-ups, the dinners, the vacations, the movies, plays, concerts, baptisms, bar-mitzvahs, funerals, the dog put down, the new dog bought, all add up to nothing. All that's happened is that time has passed. And even if this supposed life is eulogized and its biography is hailed in *The New York Times Book Review* as yet another modern masterpiece, it still adds up to zero.

A life only devoted to the cares and concerns of this world, this "mundus," is truly mundane. Such a life satisfies a certain part of us, but not the whole of us. It is one-dimensional.

But we can live in a larger, three-dimensional world. We can.

Admittedly, this mundane life of work and play and mail and fee-mail and bills and baptisms and birthdays can preoccupy us till we draw our final breath. And we may become engrossed in it and it may stimulate and stir us to hope and satisfaction, but all of that ends when we snuggle into our coffins. Such a life has only to do with this world, and to put it bluntly, this world has had enough of us.

So ends our world. We lived only for it and "it" and "I" have parted company. "It" goes on, but without us. This is the world Jesus was talking about when he said "Be in the world but not of it."

We are in the world two ways, by our physical existence and by our interest and effort. What does Jesus mean when he says to be "not of it"? If not of *it* then of what? Perhaps he means another world, a world that encompasses and infiltrates this one, a world that picks up (and picks us up) when this one is done with. He implies that we must become part of that world.

To do that, we must get a life within the life we already know.

7

To get such a life we should have to do something different than just go from one external to another, from one triviality to the next, from insignificance to insignificance. We should have to do more than drift through life in our usual way. We have to develop something inside us that can become the thread of another life. To do this we have to hold onto some of that interest and attention that is constantly being drawn out of us by each new stimulus in our everyday lives. We have to turn some of this power of attention to building a self-watchfulness, an awareness of our existence, our own livingness.

Such a person begins to develop a conscious will. What he does in this life-within-a-life is directed by his own volition. He is not blown about by the wind. He has an aim and a direction. He attends to the affairs of life knowingly, knowing what he is doing, knowing the real value of things, knowing what is real and what is unreal, what is false and what is true. He is not eaten up by the affairs of his own life. And the scope of his existence widens as it deepens. He lives in an arena larger than that of "me" and "mine" and "what's in it for me?" He goes about his business efficiently, with ease. He is about a greater business.

How to get a life within a life — that's what I teach.

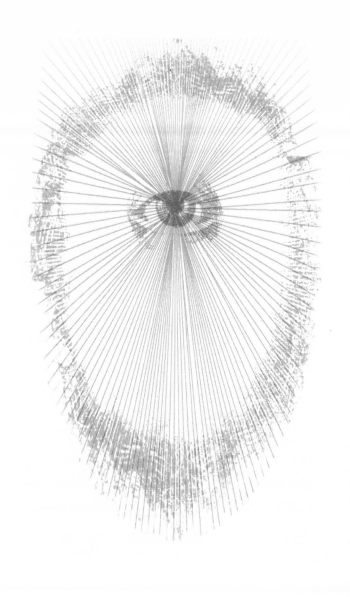

A Rope Thrown From Above

Long, long before I met Jimmy Barone I knew there was more to this world than meets the eye. I was in Mrs. Hansen's class at the time, fifth grade, P.S. 201. The genial September sun was slanting through our vast, many-paned windows, and I was walking to the Reading Table. Once we had finished our work, Mrs. Hansen invited us to choose a book. There were books galore.

But among the books there was a book that was not a book. I came across it as I was touching and smelling and thumbing my way through copies of *Robinson Crusoe, Twenty Thousand Leagues Under the Sea, Heidi, Westward Ho, Moby Dick, Swiss Family Robinson, The Lay of the Last Minstrel,* and suchlike. They were rich, appealing titles, some of them deliberately designed to set the boys giggling. But there was this *other* book, too.

I remember staring at it for a long time. It was by itself, and not among the tumbling piles. It was small. And it was white. I was transfixed. There was the face of a man on the cover and he was looking up at me.

After a while I turned aside. I picked up *Twenty Thousand Leagues Under the Sea* and tried to read the first paragraph, but my mind was on that little book. I wanted to ask Mrs. Hansen about it. What was that book? What was it about? What was it doing here? I glanced over at her. She was preoccupied, as usual. Her face bore the marks of weariness that come with being the portal for three children to enter the world. One of them, Arlene, with the platinum ringlets and turned-up nose, who sat right up front, her desk against her mother's desk, was plying the poor woman with whining questions.

Realizing I could get no help from the adult world, I forced my face to turn toward the book again. It had a title. But the title was unfathomable. *The New Testament.* What could that possibly mean? If this was the "new" testament what happened to the old one? I'd never heard of it. Besides, what in heaven's name was a testament? I was ten and I thought I knew a lot of words, but not this "testament." It sounded very important though.

As I pondered whether or not I should pick up that odd little book I noticed that as other classmates of mine wandered over to the table and began to shuffle through the books they never touched this one. They moved the books all around it but they never touched *it*. They seemed not to notice it, as if the book itself was invisible. I wondered if I was the only one who could see it.

To test its reality and to overcome my mounting anxiety, I picked the book up. I opened it, being careful not to put my fingers on the face of the man on the cover. I read something. I can't remember what it was. But I knew when I closed the book that this wasn't a book like all the other books on Mrs. Hansen's Reading Table. This wasn't a book at all. This was something different.

For the rest of the year whenever I went to the Reading Table I avoided that strange little book that wasn't really a book. Everybody else did, too, because it never changed its position on the table.

One day a madness came over me and I wanted to yell and wave my fist at Mrs. Hansen for putting that book there in the first place. I nearly did it, too. In fact, I was walking up the aisle toward her, bursting with my righteous fury when she looked up and appeared to be reminded about something.

"Oh, Frank," she said.

Then, much to my chagrin, Mrs. Hansen held up a composition of mine that had a big red A+ on it. She directed me to read it to the class as a demonstration of what a student in her class was capable of. I read it, of course, with a face as red as that A+.

Eventually, the little white book with the unblinking eyes of Christ on its cover went onto a back shelf of my mind. I stopped going to Mrs. Hansen's Reading Table; I brought my own reading matter: *The Hardy Boys* and *Nancy Drew* and their unending series of mysteries. And I felt better about things.

What I remember of religion back then, besides the little book of *The New Testament,* seems a pleasant pink haze. There were once-a-week catechism classes (called by the improbable name of "released time") and nuns and priests and crucifixes and red-covered catechism books, which raised many a question in my mind regarding things seen and unseen.

And there was a white day — with a white suit, white ribbon, white book, and white rosary beads. And not long after that a red day — nothing of which I remember but the cuff the Bishop gave my cheek. It was such an insipid slap it shocked me. (We had talked so much beforehand about how it symbolized the abuse the "confirmed" Christian had to endure.) I was lighthearted when I left the church that day, assured that life wasn't going to be as hard as I expected, but disappointed that religion had so little sting to it.

Religion was all part of the rigamarole of the adult world as far as I could tell. My parents dressed me up and sent me off to church with two nickels in my pocket, one for each collection. They never went, except on Christmas and Easter. The bells kept ringing all Sunday morning and people rushed along the avenue to get there. They rushed back home, too. And no one seemed the wiser or the better for all the sweating and dozing and dreaming and nickel-plunking. So, except for my encounter with *The New Testament* on Mrs. Hansen's Reading Table, what passed for religion seemed oh-so-dull and oh-so-ordinary, until I met Jimmy Barone.

Each block in Brooklyn was so much an entity unto itself that I had never known Jimmy even though he only lived one block away. He was a bit of a loner, determined to succeed at something; in contrast, I was always in the middle of a milling throng, dubious about success in any form. We both landed up on the track team. He because he wanted to win races, and I because I was a fast runner and pathetically naïve.

Here's how it happened: I'm in high school, at last, liberated from elementary school. And we have gym classes — with bars you can swing on, with mats you can roll on, with ropes you can climb, up to a thirty-foot ceiling. Then one day early in the year word goes out that we're going outside, and we're going to have races! This is right up my alley. I'm a speed demon. I'm the fastest kid in the neighborhood. I give guys a two-sewer lead and I still beat them. I love to run. I figured we're running for the fun of it, for the delight of having the wind whizzing by our ears, for the glory of fleet feet.

In reality, we were running because Mr. Brown, the cadaverous track coach, was scouting prospects. So I win, and I win, and I win again. And before the day is out I succumb to Mr. Brown's flattery and oily promises.

The track team took all the joy out of running. I hated it like I hated Listerine. I cut as often as I could, till Brown caught up with me and threatened me with not graduating. I had to graduate because college was my liberation from the horror of high school. So I stuck with it and that's how I got to know Jimmy, which is probably the real reason I ended up on the track team. Destiny works that way.

We used to walk home together after practice, talking about one thing or another. Jimmy didn't smile much. He had a chin that jutted out and he walked hunched over, his legs kicking out like a wooden soldier's. His feet were pointed out like a duck's. He was a lousy runner but persistent. And I liked him.

One day he started talking about religion. The streets were pretty empty except for the swarming gnats that came with the season. It was October, a warm afternoon, the whole world gone soft and ripe. The old Italians were making their wine and you could smell their grapes in the air. Jimmy was just talking at first, asking me questions about what I believed in, and then, as we turned up 80th Street, he dropped the bombshell. He wasn't a Catholic anymore. He had given it up. He had found true religion.

I was aghast. How could he do such a thing? We were Catholics. That's what we *were*. We couldn't just go around changing. Even though the religion I was born into didn't mean anything to me it suddenly seemed so important and sacred. Jimmy's decision was a betrayal of something … of everything! But I didn't say any of this. I listened mostly. Jimmy had never spoken with such fervor before and the whole subject seemed wildly interesting.

During the next year or two I saw Jimmy a lot — outside of the track team. I went over to his house and studied with him and his family, who had all somehow "converted." Despite my trepidation, I went to some talks at a local hall, and, lifted on a crest of interest, I went with Jimmy to Yankee Stadium to witness one Nathan Knorr speak about Armageddon.

As far as I was concerned, Yankee Stadium was not the best place for a religious convention. I was a Dodger fan and the damn Yankees had inflicted such suffering upon us that I loathed anything connected to them — their uniforms, their players, Mel Allen, and of course, the stadium. But I was looking for the truth, and nothing was going to stop me.

Well, as luck would have it, Nathan Knorr didn't say a thing despite the three hours he took to say it. The biblical quotations the beastly stadium resounded with were just quotes that added up to anything you wanted them to add up to. Printed matter floated around copiously, carrying as much significance as dry leaves before a flood. I looked but I didn't find the truth, at least not where I was supposed to see it.

I did find it though, and the impact of it is still with me. It was *in the people;* that's where the truth was. The people there, those Jehovah's Witnesses in Yankee Stadium, were flushed with kindness and love and brotherhood and the longing for a finer life. And I've never found their spirit anywhere else, not in the church I grew up in, not in the churches I visited, not in groups, not in schools, not among priests nor the supposed holy ones. The Witnesses, with all their irritating door-knockings and black bags and Watchtowers and refusing transfusions and Army service, they had the truth of religion alive in them.

That's how I came to understand what religion really was. Not the externals, the dogmas, but a *possibility* flung down to us from a higher, finer world. That possibility we could, if we wished, actualize here, now, in this hard and heedless world. Love, for instance, comes from above. What we call love is either biological (family, blood) or social (people who happen to be doing the same thing at the same time) or alchemical (boy loves girl). All earth-level love. This other love — love for all — is from a higher level. Such love is possible to realize and live; I've seen it. I've felt it.

This is the picture that comes to me: a hole cut in the invisible ceiling between this world and the one above, like the hole a fisherman cuts in the ice to connect to the fish-world below. But instead of the line and baited hook the fisherman uses to yank up fish, whoever cuts the hole above us throws down a rope. This rope, which is the connector to the finer world, is not for pulling us up, but for us to climb, hand over hand, with our feet gripping the place we've attained, until we reach the heaven of our hearts.

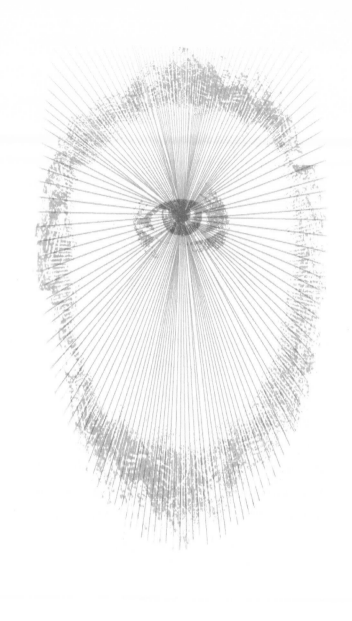

To Work or Not to Work

Since there's no point to pretense except on the stage, I must confess to you that I wasn't always the paragon of virtue that I am today. This, I suspect, comes as no surprise to many. Yes, indeed, I was once so without honor that my own father (bless his forthright tongue) declared me a "lazy bum." Of course, I never thought of myself that way.

At the time he spoke those words, I was a college student, and as my undeniable Dad put it "You think the world owes you a living." Which was true. As far as I could tell, ever since I was a child, I had no reason to think otherwise. What made my father's judgement so hard to swallow was the fact that he had provided me with that living and was continuing to do so at that very moment.

He was torn. As a second generation Italian he didn't want his son to earn a living digging ditches; therefore I needed to get an education. But he recognized the attitude that my lopsided education engendered (and which I was absorbing all too well) was turning me into a sponger, and an ungrateful one at that. All he could do was rail against my unvarnished indolence.

What I didn't see then but see now is this: I was all in my head. And my head was full of dreams. "My work is supposed to be to study," was my defense, although, if the truth be known, I did as little of that as I could, usually waiting for the last minute and doing just enough to get by. I wasn't much of a student, using up the maximum cuts and absences, taking no notes, cracking a book only when doom was looking me in the eye, spending most of my time rambling in the library stacks, following a whimsical course of reading, conversing with pretty girls, and drowsing by the goldfish pond. I never told my father that, preferring to keep up the appearance of an overburdened scholar lugging weighty tomes back and forth to school. They were building my biceps, I told myself.

The "school" I went to was Brooklyn College, which has, somewhat miraculously, since become part of a university. Back then, it was known as a subway college, without forms or dorms. I rode the New York City Rapid Transit Line — the bus — back and forth each day. This only increased my propensity to daydream, for to have one's carcass transported to-and-from the halls of education only furthers drowsiness and passivity. Ultimately, ingratitude and disrespect for the whole process sets in, like mildew. But it was either "get an education" or go to work, and I dreaded *that* even more.

Yes, I was lazy, ambitionless, a model freeloader and yet as I look back at it, that wasn't the whole story. Frankly, I didn't see anything worth doing, worth working *for.* No doubt, if I had to work or starve I would have done something. But I didn't have to, so I malingered in the halls of poison ivy as long as I could.

The thought of work and the why of it hounded me. Why had God, in Genesis, made it such a curse? After kicking Adam out of Paradise He sentenced the poor fellow to work by the sweat of his brow. I wondered: was it God who really dumped this on us or was it man's attitude that put the words in God's mouth? Everywhere I looked people were just drudging along. Most people lived for their vacations. They hated their job; they were always looking for another job, a better job, an easier job. They suffered through their job till the weekend so they could do what they really wanted to do — usually some senseless "recreational activity." Some didn't vegetate on their days off, or go scampering off to some fool's game; some had hobbies — collecting junk, or making doorstops in their basement shops. Nobody liked work.

Even my father didn't really like it. He did it. He did it valiantly. He rarely missed a day; he had to be practically dying not to go in. He worked the night shift most of his life. He slept for seven hours, got up, worked around the house fixing things, and, since he was a skilled printer, did odd jobs on his basement printing press: wedding invitations and business cards, whatever people needed. He couldn't stop working. He couldn't stand sitting around. Right through the Depression, he was never out of work. He was admirable. He took care of us. He wore himself out. He didn't have much of a life.

I probably wouldn't have lifted a finger to do any work at all if I hadn't come across that midnight-green Cadillac. Convertible, plush red leather and carpeting, fins on the rear fenders, she purred like a sweet, salacious pantheress. Caressing that Cadillac sent me looking for a job, drove me, against my will, to the Great Atlantic & Pacific Tea Company on 13th Avenue to face the ogre — Hugo Tortorella.

Hugo was a legend in the neighborhood, in the annals of the Tea Company and beyond. Napoleonic, handsome, blue-eyed behind hexagonal rimless eyeglasses, he always wore a suit or sports jacket, white shirt and a prim-and-prissy bow tie. He drove his staff relentlessly. He was all over the store, always in motion. You never knew where he was lurking, or where he would next appear. He expected his people to earn their dollars.

Hugo was a terror.

Fat Steve recommended me for the job. Steve was a friend who liked to make money. He'd been luring me to work there with tales of all the fun we'd have at the A&P. Eventually, the idea was for all the guys on the block to get jobs at the A&P and we'd be all together having the same great time we always had except the Tea Company would be paying us. I didn't buy it, but when the Caddy came along, she turned my head. So with Fat Steve backing me (and Hugo loved Steve) Hugo took a look at me and gave me the nod. I was in.

Before I went in that Thursday, in my dreams I had banked all the cash I needed and was cruising the neighborhood with the Caddy's top down and a blonde beside me. Everything was working out perfectly. That first evening Al, the assistant manager, was on duty and he hardly noticed me. I bumbled about, trying not to look too stupid, or too inept. I was bored. I hardly saw Steve. It was a long four hours.

Though that first night had dampened my enthusiasm, I didn't realize what a mistake I had made until the next day of work. It was a Saturday. I met Hugo on my way in. I was 17 minutes late.

Now, I was used to being late. It was a badge of honor to be late at school. It showed a scholarly scorn for the subject at hand and for all the flummery of higher education.

But Hugo didn't see things that way. He raged and fumed and it looked for a while like my Cadillac dreams were doomed.

"I'm going to give you *one more chance*, Crocitto," he snarled. That's how Saturday began. For nine interminable hours Hugo harassed me, ridiculed and chased me, insulted me and sent me downstairs to the dairy and to produce and up front to bag and back on the floor. I thought I was the only guy working the store. Mine was the only name he shouted over the p.a. system.

"Crocitto! Up front!"

"Crocitto! Unload the delivery truck!"

"Crocitto! To the butcher!"

I was humiliated.

And he didn't want me to just walk wherever he sent me; he wanted me to power-walk there. Hugo invented the power-walk. He'd have me power-walk to the butcher, where there was a walk-in freezer and all I had on was a summer shirt. Dead cows hanging on hooks, chicken guts everywhere. There were people in the freezer, all bundled up against the cold, their breath smoky in front of their faces and I had to scrape up the fat off the floor, unload barrels, hump heavy wet boxes like a coolie — quick-sticks — always rushing, because Hugo was calling my name on the loudspeaker again.

One of the people all bundled up there loading pork into a sausage machine was a gorgeous blonde. And she was giggling and glancing at me and whispering to her friend. Giggling intolerably.

"Crocitto! On the floor!"

So, I finished humping the meat boxes into the freezer and sprinted out onto the floor. There in Aisle 3 Hugo showed me the enemy — a long, tan line of boxes stacked high as a line of basketball players, boxes full of canned goods that I had to empty single-handedly.

"They're all yours, Crocitto," Hugo crowed,

slapping my back. I gasped and began.

I worked. Or rather I thought I was working. Hugo said I was counting the cans. Then he demonstrated how he wanted me to do it. He wanted me to throw the cans onto the shelf like a popcorn popper. I tried, but I still had no idea how slow I was.

At last, the big hand moved to the twelve and the little hand moved to the six. The clock had had to fight its way through molasses to reach six o'clock. I smiled for the first time that day. But I still had an hour to go, and Hugo had one more job for me up the natty sleeve of his sport jacket.

We had to do the floors, me and Henny, a Norwegian kid with one arm. That meant we had to sweep the whole, indescribable vastness of the store, and then, since the floors were wooden, we had to spread oil onto them and when the wood had soaked up the oil sufficiently we spread some strange, fragrant, sawdust-like stuff called feldspar on it and after the feldspar had soaked up the ex-

34

cess oil, Henny and I swept the whole store again.

It took an hour, with Hugo goading and harassing us and comparing us to men working under water. I gritted my teeth and bent my back, growing more and more nauseated by the stink of the feldspar. Through it all I tried to hang on to the value of such a thing as a Cadillac, a task which proved as elusive as the smile of a Cheshire cat.

But, as I worked, something let go inside me and I stopped caring about the weariness of my muscles, about Cadillacs and blondes, about what I could have been doing instead of what I was doing, about time and how it was being eaten up moment by moment. I even stopped caring about Hugo and what he thought of me. I found myself just working.

It was the oddest thing: I was working and watching myself work and I had no motive any longer. My only motive was I wanted to do it. I felt free and exhilarated. It was like flying must be if you're a bird. I had, despite myself — my reluctance, my resentment, my preferences — stepped into the world of men, the world of work. This was why men worked; and I was one with them all. The elixir of joy was running through my heart. My eyes were moist with gratitude. I was ready and willing to work all night. Mostly I was grateful to Hugo Tortorella.

That was my first day with Hugo. Little did I know I was to have two more years with him. At the end of my tenure at the A&P, he didn't want to let me go. I kept trying to quit and go on to something else, but he kept giving me raises. I had gotten very fast; I had become his main part-timer. I could power-walk as well as he could.

Eventually we parted. He hugged me the same way he did after the oiling and feldsparring of the floors — one arm around my shoulders, his head looking away, with his other hand rubbing his knuckles into my ribs. Then he went off to his office — full speed — as if his office were on fire.

My father's gone. Hugo Tortorella is probably

gone, too. Wherever they are they must be having a good giggle at the irony of it all. You see, the subject I teach and have worked at these many years is often called the "Work."

And, damn it, it is.

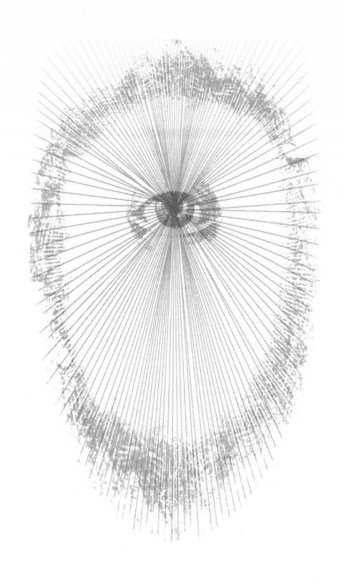

The Great
Midnight-Green Cadillac

If there's to be an article on cars then there's nothing for it but to tell the tale of The Great Midnight-Green Cadillac. Other stories of other cars might entertain. Even assorted episodes with some of Brooklyn's notorious grease monkeys might do. My exploits with "Joe," the Mechanic of Mechanics, who could diagnose car trouble solely by ear and never dirtied his hands would be amusing and enlightening, but they will all have to wait till another time. This, though, the saga of the Great Midnight-Green Cadillac, is so packed with agony and ecstasy it stands in a class by itself. It is the only real car story worth telling.

The story has its roots in the early, pre-license

hankerings of a teenager's soul. Since, as the *Bhagavad-Gita* says, desires arise out of what we are ever looking at, gawking at, and admire, I and my friends were foredoomed. In Brooklyn we had eyes only for cars and girls and cherished wild hopes to one day have both in the palm of one hand. Car keys were the key to everything. We'd lean against the corner fence or drape over the parking meters and with lustful languor watch the cars zoom by along the Avenue. We gazed and yearned for cars of our own.

The automobile was the vehicle of liberation. With wheels we could get out of the neighborhood, out of the gridwork of streets and avenues, out of the bulging flabby sprawl of the borough, out of the metal-hearted clutches of New York City into the lovely, leafy land of "Upstate," where there were lakes and mountains and air and trees and roads that led to glorious places all over the nation. With wheels we could chauffeur girls who were weary of walking, beautiful girls who loved to smile and let their haloed tresses wave in the sweet breeze. And even if we didn't have enough money for gas (25 cents a gallon) to go on major excursions into the hinterlands, we could roar along the streets of Brooklyn, but above it all, like gods or some such superior beings.

So, we suffered through the long years reaching, stretching toward the blessed age of eighteen. We heard of places where kids got licenses at sixteen, and we wished somehow we could get to live there, but we knew in our hearts we were in bondage to Brooklyn. We waited and we dreamed of the new life that would be ours with a license-to-drive and a car, a car to drive. Eventually, all agonies come to an end. Eventually we all became eighteen.

A permit came first, then the practice, then the test. Before the test, all was speculation, uncertainty:

Sometimes they fail you the first time.

Sometimes they don't like you.

Sometimes they fail you because they don't want too many kids on the road.

Sometimes they just fail you.

Sweating under my arms, my hands a-tremor, I went, on time, to the spot on Fort Hamilton Parkway where you lined up to be tested. The written test was a breeze; the road test was the killer. The examiner issued commands; I obeyed. He jotted things down. No conversation. Parallel park! I backed in. Perfect — in one move. I got it on my first shot: I had a license!

So, having neither money nor job, I decided to buy a car. I wanted a car. I had to have a car. I didn't care — even if it was gray. And it turned out to be gray, a dull, unshineable gray. I bought it off a teacher, an ashen-faced gray man, for thirty-five dollars. A four-door Dodge, gray inside and out.

It was a beginning.

No one was impressed by my car. My father referred to it as "The Shebang." Though I invoked the ancient justification for ugly, dumpy vehicles: "It may not look good but it gets me there," I was secretly dissatisfied and began scheming how to unload it for something prestigious. The car I was looking for was around somewhere, but I had a shortage of funds. The shortage forced me to go to work at the A&P. Glumly, I calculated that I could amass enough to upgrade ... in two years.

About this time Joe Panz and I had become good friends. Joe Panz (short for Panzera) and I met in high school. He was a good student, liked to joke, relished adventures, the kind of guy it was easy to pal around with. He was tall as me but with broad shoulders and a lot more meat on him. His face was like a baby's, round and smooth, with cherub-rouged cheeks. He was desperate for a car.

One day I proposed a plan to Joe Panz. We could be partners. Together, we'd buy a couple of cars, cars for different occasions. I had the gray one already, good if you didn't want to impress anybody, like if we had to go to a funeral, or something — when you didn't want to stand out. Next we could get something a little more flashy, like a red roadster with dual exhausts. Something good for showing off in. There were endless possibilities. We could even get a nice car, eventually. We could have a whole fleet. Joe didn't have a job at the time but he liked the idea, and we sealed our partnership with a handshake.

Motivated, Joe came to work at the A&P with me and half of the other guys on 81st Street, working under the exacting leadership of the aforementioned Hugo Tortorella. Though Joe hadn't paid a penny on the dull, gray Dodge, I let him drive it around. Meanwhile we looked around for something hotter. Joe didn't like the work much, and Hugo didn't like his work much so Joe didn't work much. But dollar by dollar he bought his way into the partnership.

I think he had paid me seven dollars towards his share of the Dodge when we came upon the car we'd been dreaming about. It was parked right outside the Nineteenth Hole, a watering place near the Dyker Park Golf Course. Bright, shiny, and crouched in a posture of speed was a Ford roadster. And it was for sale. Two full seats in front, a crunched seat in back and a rumble seat outside. What a car! The owner, a weasel-faced bartender called Johnny Q, wanted $125 but we got him down to $115. Joe had $9.50 and I had the rest. (Things were financially a little uneven at the time.) He was apologetic and even suggested that we wait till he saved some more, but I didn't want to lose the car. I'd never seen anything like it.

"Let's just get it," I said. "We'll worry about it later."

"I'm with you, Cicce," Joe said.

We were fast friends. I wasn't concerned about the money.

When we came roaring down 81st on our maiden ride a crowd gathered. Everybody wanted to drive it. But we decided we couldn't take a chance with the insurance danger. So we *gave* people rides. That was our policy, only *we* drive, Joe and me.

"That's it. You wanna ride? Get in."

It was the kind of car you couldn't help petting. We were on our way to assembling a fleet. The only drawback to "Flaming Red" was she didn't climb hills very well, but we didn't have many hills in Brooklyn anyway. Joe and I never talked about it. I worried about it though, enough to show it to my Uncle Vito who got a very gloomy look on his face (he had been a mechanic from Day One) and he spoke one of those words a person doesn't like to hear:

"*Compression*. It's got no compression."

My heart sank, but I kept my face implacable. Then he sang the song that I've heard many times since.

> *Why didn't you tell me you wanted to buy a car?*
> *I could have gotten you a good car.*
> *The guy next door had this beautiful, immaculate Mercury.*

But he just sold it. Beautiful.
No comparison.
You should have told me.

I had a knack for always buying the wrong thing, always just missing the deal of a lifetime.

Compression or no compression, I took "Flaming Red" everywhere. Even into Jersey. The time that sticks most in my mind is when a bunch of us headed out towards Dover to go to work in the kitchen of a summer camp run by Benedictine monks. We'd gotten off to a late start so we wound up hitting the hills as night was casting a purply cloak over everything. I was uneasy driving in the dark. We were coming down a hill at a fast clip, about 65 mph, which was a little too fast considering that the brakes were low and the tires were close to being bald. I was driving and I couldn't keep the speed between 50 and 60 because the steering wheel shook too much. I was holding it real tight so nobody would see how much it was shaking. We had a carload. Once I got over 60, the steering wheel calmed down, but I began to have flashing visions of my front tires flying off. I needed the greater speed in order to get up the next hill. As we neared the bottom of the hill, I gave it a little extra gas; we went up to 70. Then something happened that I had never experienced before. I had the pedal to the floor but it felt like the car wasn't going any faster. It seemed, in fact, to be slowing up. And it did slow up, rapidly. My right foot was mashing the floorboard but "Red" wasn't getting any gas. There was gas in the tank though. So I pulled over, amid a hullabaloo from the carload.

The emergency brake wouldn't hold so I turned the car off, locking us in gear. We all sat in the silence for a while. And I thought of my Uncle Vito and the Mercury he could have gotten for me and the mysteries of compression.

"What do we do now?" somebody said. Somebody always says that.

"Anybody got a flashlight?" Joe Panz said.

By some miracle, feeling in the dark through all the luggage produced a flashlight. The light was feeble but sufficient to take a quick look. The gas pedal was slack, flapping like a broken wing.

The thought that we'd been driving in a car (and that I had actually bought a car) whose gas pedal could just come undone was even more depressing than the reality of being stranded in the dark hills of Jersey. Pitch-black hills. Except for an occasional car going by you'd never imagine there had ever been something called light.

Joe Panz, in admirable optimism, got out and went under the car. There were large holes in the floor so we could see his face, dimly lit by the flash, looking up at us.

"You know anything about cars, Joe?" somebody said.

"Who's idea was this?"

"That flashlight's not gonna last."

"You see anything, Joe?"

"I think I see something," Joe said. He was

groaning and shifting.

"You should always put fresh batteries in a flashlight before you go anywhere," someone proclaimed.

"Did *you!*?"

"I didn't bring a flashlight."

And so the conversation went until the light from the flashlight faded and died in those black hills of western New Jersey.

"Now what?"

"I might be able to do this by feel," Joe muttered.

"Yeah, Joe's good at feeling things up, right Joe?"

Joe didn't seem in the mood for joking, especially after some oil dropped in the center of his forehead. We listened to Joe Panz grunting and spitting in the dark and every once in a while speculating as to where that oil drop could have come from.

Then suddenly things lit up. A car coming in

our direction threw its headlight beams into the car but more importantly *under* the car so that Joe could actually see what he was doing for a few seconds. There was another long dark wait and then a car and then another wait, and then three cars in a row running like pack rats on each other's tails. As the last string of pack rats passed Joe spoke quietly.

"I got it."

And he did. We heard him snapping something into place, and squirming his way out from under. In the dark, we felt him glowing like a drunken angel when he climbed back in.

"Do I know something about cars, or do I know something about cars?" Joe snickered.

Later on, after the summer sank into the irretrievable past, to complicate our partnership even further I insisted that we needed a Vespa, a motor scooter, with a side car. The scooter worked out all right, though the side car, unbalancing the whole affair, gave us two close calls.

Both times I was in the sidecar. Oh, yes, there was a third time too.

The disadvantage of having more than one vehicle on the road is that you never know when you'll crash into your own car, or it into you. The third close call came when I decided to scoot up the block, defying the ONE WAY signs. There were no cars coming, so it didn't seem much of a risk. Except, when I got near the corner, a big, shiny midnight-green Cadillac came wheeling around the turn with Joe Panz at the helm. I leapt off the scooter. He missed me by inches. Joe "barely tapped it," he said. The scooter kept going and plowed into a nearby johnny-pump, interrupting the business of a big lion-maned chow who was majestically urinating on it at the time.

I should have taken that incident as a sign of things to come. For a lot was coming. Which leads me to the point of all this: The Great Midnight-Green Cadillac.

Joe had heard about it. I don't know how. Perhaps his brother who was a cop had learned of it. We planned to go look at it, against both our parents' emphatic advice. It was in a garage on Atlantic Avenue. So we went.

The car was the kind of car that makes a person forget about words and become a gazer, an admirer, a captive. It had an effect similar to that of the gorgeous ladies of the screen like Lana Turner and Hedy Lamarr and Ava Gardner. There she was: relaxed and sleek as a giant cat. She sat in sphinx-like repose, waiting. Waiting for Joe and me. Immaculate was the word for her. Not a scratch. Elegant dark green, with fins, those subtle fins of the early Cadillacs, before they became a caricature of themselves. Gentle, subtle, dignified fins. Red leather seats, dark red carpeting, thick and lush, hardly scuffed. Convertible, too.

We pretended disinterest as the salesman, a gangly guy in a suit with a face like lemon meringue pie with five o'clock shadow showed us the 1948 Cadillac's main features, her all too obvious blandishments. Our hearts were beating. I was rehearsing how I would present this godsend to my Aunt Grace, the only member of my family who could sometimes be cajoled into bankrolling my schemes. I came up with pages of self-abasing dialogue. I groveled. I made exorbitant promises. Anything and everything to make it impossible for her to say no. She was my one and only hope. She was *our* only hope.

Whether a price is high or low depends on how much you want a thing. When I first heard "six hundred dollars" I gasped and blacked out for a moment. An enormous sum, not only to me and Joe, but enormous at that time in history. But after we'd rode in it, or rather, floated in it, and we heard the so-seductive purring of that great cat, it didn't seem quite so much. The more we talked of it on the way home the more it seemed a bargain. When I got before my Aunt Grace, a kind, lovely woman who put up with me and my schemes for far too long, I was a flaming pillar of sincerity: I told her it was a steal, the steal of a lifetime.

It took a week. She had to think about it. She laughed at first, and dismissed the whole idea. What concerned her most was not the payment, or would Joe and I be sufficiently responsible, but that my mother — her sister — would find out that she had lent me the money.

"She'll kill me," Aunt Grace declared in her raspy voice.

"She won't kill you, believe me. I'll never tell her."

"She'll figure it out," she said.

"No, she won't."

"She will. Who else would be crazy and stupid and idiotic enough to lend you money?"

"We'll pay you. I swear."

We spoke about it every day. Until she got so mad at me she threw me out of her living room. The next day she said yes.

That was the beginning of the triumph, the

achievement of the ages. I, at the age of 18, owned a Cadillac. The best of all possible Cadillacs — the Great Midnight-Green Cadillac! Little did I know where great triumphs lead.

We drove it out of the garage. We drove it so carefully, so slowly — like we were in a ticker-tape parade — that drivers honked at us all the way home. Fears set in almost immediately: somebody might slash the canvas top; it may leak when it rains. It's going to be cold in the winter. It guzzles high-test. (The meringue-faced salesman, in the oily way of an undertaker, had reminded us of that as we drove off.) We had the *car*, but now we had to maintain it. Joe was exuberant. I was preoccupied, and could barely muster a smile as we drove up to my house.

Gradually I shook off my fears and began to enjoy the great car. The smoothness of the ride was like cruising down a hallway of wall-to-wall carpeting. She was too grand a car to simply ride around the streets; she cried out for the open road.

I rode out to Canarsie once with Nancy who worked in the butcher shop. She had real blond hair and she laughed all the way there. She looked ravishing. And the Caddy seemed created to transport her beauty. When we stopped on the pier, where the gang used to go crabbing, and began to talk and smooch, the glamour quickly faded. Nancy was nice, but she was so simple she made me feel sorry for her. I never asked her out again.

Once I took a long trip past Ellenville, up north in Ulster County, to a bungalow colony where my folks and my sister and brother were staying. I rode through the night into the dawn and got there when the dew was sparkling on the grass and the blackbirds were going wild among the blueberry bushes.

Nothing is perfect. So, too, with Cadillacs. This one, we soon discovered to our sadness, had an oil leak. After pumping up our courage, we went to see old pie-puss, determined to bully him into fixing it. He agreed without a struggle and without a smile. Three weeks out of a glorious summer passed before it was ready. And it still leaked. So we took it back. It took another week before it was really fixed and then he handed us a bill for a hundred and fifty dollars. We settled on twenty-five. And he told us never to come back. We had no intention of ever doing so.

Summer came and went and then came fall. We rode with the top down most of the time. It was a carefree time. People asked me where I got the money to buy such a car. I laughed, for I knew I didn't have the money and that a person could buy things without really having the money. And that was before credit cards. Some people wait all their lives and never have a Cadillac of their own. Some only ride in one at their funeral. "I'm not going to wait for my funeral to ride in one," I'd say. I thought I was swift in those days.

I didn't use it much that winter. The heater made it warm enough but it seemed drafty and I had a lot of school work. But when the spring came round I was ready to go places. We, Joe and I, had sold the scooter and the other two cars. So we had to plan when we each wanted to use the Caddy. I mean *I* had to plan because Joe always seemed to *need* the car. Sometimes a week went by, or more, when I didn't even see the car. What made matters worse was Joe's inability to come up with his share of the weekly payment to my Aunt; I was shouldering the whole thing.

Sometimes you see a thing coming and you don't want to see it. Maybe that's why so many people got hit by trains in the old days. I saw it coming. We argued about the unequal use of the car. He acknowledged it, after a long, hard two hours. He also agreed to come up with his share. Yet, little by little I saw less and less of Joe. He always seemed to be busy, and he always seemed to need the car. He had a girlfriend.

"And you know how much time that takes, Cicce..." he said. But who she was he never said.

Before long, I found out. She was a fat girl.

59

Maybe fat is not right — she was a big, somewhat formless girl, from 16th Avenue. She was the kind of girl who had a face that you kept expecting to become pretty and a body that would someday get some shape to it. She was about 15. Joe was 19. They said Joe was robbing the cradle, but people used to say that a lot. Her name was Teresa. Personally I was ashamed of him for taking up with her. I wouldn't give her a second look, but she was the one for Joe.

She was the one in more ways than one. And I found out which way she was the one, one afternoon after I came home from school. All my friends knew about it. And they all wanted to know if I had heard about it. I hadn't. They had. They told me.

My friend Joe had taken Teresa for a ride. Last night. And he had let her drive the car. The Great Midnight-Green Convertible Cadillac. That great, beautiful car, that one-of-a-kind. That immaculate magnificent piece of perfection. And so she had come around the corner of my very own block at about two in the morning, hit a car, skinned it and went on from there to another and another and only after hitting six parked cars was she able to conclude her evening's performance.

"She wanted to drive the car," Joe told me, in whining explanation.

"But why? I just want to know why. Why?"

He answered and he talked and I think he nearly cried, but there was no why. It was just one of those things, one of those irrational things.

I remember looking at the car, all smashed on its right side, the fender and the door, all the way to the back fin, and wondering how things could happen the way they do. Joe had gotten an appraisal, something like $250 to $300, but I half heard. It didn't matter to me. The Great Midnight-Green Cadillac was no more.

It left a wake though. The repairs had to be done and the repairs had to be paid for and Joe didn't have any money, although he promised to

see if he could get some. And we still owed about
$425 on it. And we had to go through the repairs
in order to sell the damn thing.

When it came back from the shop, as good as
new, as they say, I could barely look at it. I knew
the dents and scratches were still there, I could
feel them underneath the putty and the paint. We
sold it, for $400. Joe could never seem to come
up with any more money for my Aunt, so I paid
the rest. I saw Joe once or twice after that. And
that was the last I ever saw him.

For me, now, cars are just to ride in. None of
them impress me. I once rode in the Great Midnight-Green Cadillac Convertible. And I owned
it ... for a while.

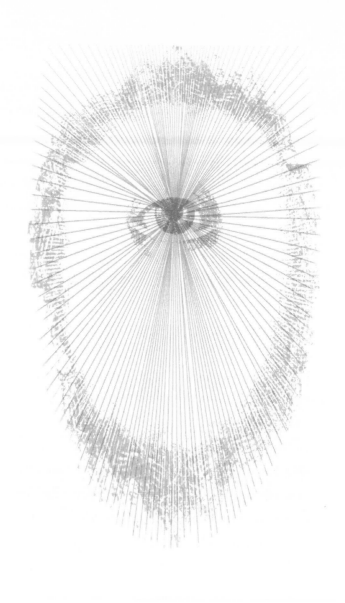

Me and Michelangelo
(Pronounced "Mee-kell-*an*-jello")

My life as a sculptor began when I was an un-
beaten beatnik in my early twenties. I was living
on a farm on Staten Island with a bunch of bums
who were trying to beat the system. One day,
"hair-cut day" came around, and because I was
there and because there was a free pair of scissors,
somebody dared me to have a go at it. Scrawny,
scraggly, scabby, and graceless though my first cli-
ent was, in half an hour he had a beautiful head.
Word rose up among the disconsolate that I had
"the gift." And I did. I do. I knew after the first
haircut that I would never go hungry. I could always paint a pole with red white and blue stripes
and set up shop. So, over the years I've snipped
and snacked a few heads.

Little did I know I was not to make my fortune as a barber, but as a teacher. My friends tell me I've always been teaching. I used to teach on the street corners in Brooklyn, year round, even in the bitter cold when we'd huddle around the shoulders of a building, stamping and shaking to keep warm. I just did it. I had the gift. I suppose I came stepping out of the womb teaching. And if all goes according to plan I'll probably be instructing the fellow in black undertaking me to my tomb. We all do what we can't help doing.

Now you might ask what does barbering or pedagogy have to do with sculpting? And I might reply that except for the difference in density of the raw materials, these three arts are about the same. Each aims at creating order out of disorder, at giving shape to the shapeless, at turning darkness into light, ugliness into beauty, grossness into grace. Differences there are, of course. A head, situated atop the neck of someone who's willing to give you his back, is trustful, willing and accepting. With only occasional reassurances, aided by a mirror, such a person will sit out the session and arise from the chair all the better-trimmed and resplendent.

A stone, too, is pliant, patient, responsive. Though reputedly inert, hard and unconscious, it takes the whack of the hammer and chisel patiently, respectfully. Whatever cuts and inroads are made remain so. You get no rejection or backsliding from a stone. More than that, a stone asks for more. A stone exults in the removal of what is unnecessary.

Not so a student. I've used jackhammers and 60-pound sledges; I've dynamited and sandblasted; I've levered and lasered, mostly to no avail. A head of hair, though it grows back, recalls its former glory; a stone never forgets; a pupil rarely remembers.

Sculpting is easy. Maybe like cutting hair and forming the recalcitrant, it comes easy because I'm Italian. Because my hand and eye know a beautiful shape. This comes with the blood. Even when I set out to sculpt an ugly face, it comes out beautiful.

Carving a stone is the quintessential art. This hard, immovable, lifeless chunk must be wrestled with, stripped bare and breathed into until it comes alive. Devoted, sustained, attentive efforts eventually succeed and lo, where there had been a nondescript hunk of rock there now stands a living stone.

The funny thing is, a stone brought to life has more life than most fleshly things. The life in the *David* overwhelms, overawes and overshadows the poor, petty onlookers who pass beneath its gaze. Not only that, its life goes on — immortal, that is, as long as the stone lasts. The sculptor pours his life, his soul, into the stone. The days, the years of gazing and feeling and chipping and sanding and polishing bring about this anima-transfer. Sometimes the sculptor gets the shock of his life when he sees his life looking back at him from the stone he has been hammering at. It seems more alive

68

than he. Falling in love with a stone is the root of the idol-worship that was such a temptation in the old Semitic world.

Michelangelo was working on himself as he worked on that lean piece of Carrara marble. He poured his very life out of himself and into *David*. He gave his life and thereby had it more abundantly. He became greater than *David*. He made himself more immortal than stone. He became an Immortal.

After all, we form ourselves by whatever we do. Whatever becomes of us depends on what we do and how we do it. Baking bread, driving a car, ice-skating — it doesn't matter, we're working on the substances of the world and with each stroke we shape ourselves. We can end up non-entities or we can become immortal beings.

Viewed this way, living in the glorious medium of this world is art, requires art, results in art. Sculpting is just the most direct road. If you don't believe me, ask Michelangelo when you see him.

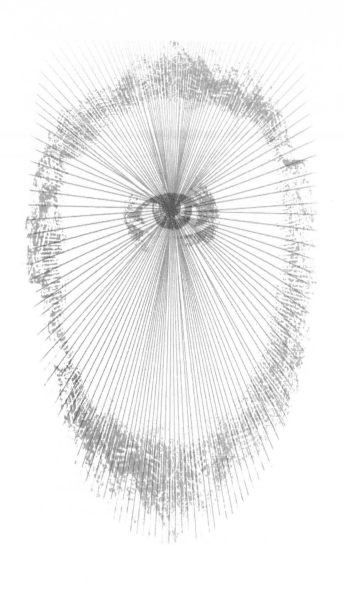

Affidavit of an Outsider

Things were so bad I was seeing double and in the merciless desolation of three in the morning, listening to the grinding gears of mail trucks and garbage trucks and the screel of an occasional cat in the alley, smoking alone on the fire escape of a cockroach-ridden apartment in Greenwich Village, I toyed with the idea of "ending it." But I didn't. I wouldn't take action, for I couldn't trust my own judgment. So I kept smoking and dragging on, doing the things we do called living — eating and sleeping and brushing teeth and washing body, going upstairs and down, indoors and out, scratching and yawning ...

Insight is Better Than Ice Cream

The last time my eyes had double vision was when I was 12 and had polio and they rushed me in a howling ambulance through the coal-black night to a hospital where I was supposed to die. I didn't die then either. But I had the same feeling of futility.

Heavy and aimless, I trudged through the double-vision days of my thirty-third year. I was supposed to have accomplished great things by that time; that's what they had predicted for me in school. But I could not get my bearings. I didn't know where I was supposed to be going, so how could I get my bearings? Bearings to what destination? All my friends, and less-than-friends, all, to a man, had jobs and professions and directions. They were all moving on the swelling wave of success. Doctors, lawyers, actors, writers. They had all left me behind.

Reading, dreaming and watching movies was my only solace. For a little while I could forget the hopelessness that hemmed me in. But when I could no longer control the focus of my eyes, I had no escape. Yet, though I say I had no hope, I must have had some, a little grain maybe, because I kept on breathing and I kept on wishing that something would transpire and it would all change and I would feel alive again like when I was a little boy commanding the waters of the mighty Verrazano Bay, striding under the sun and building castles of delight out of sand.

An analysis of my problem was not beyond me, nor was it so profound. I had simply lost all sense of meaning. Nothing mattered; nothing meant anything. Though I was living in "The Big Town," "The City That Never Sleeps," "The Big Apple" and all that rot, I could find nothing of value, nothing I could give my heart to, nothing I could throw my life's energy into. Cabs full of people raced down the streets of New York. Where were they rushing to? Subway cars were packed at rush hour. Where were all these people going and what were they doing when they got there?

Insight is Better Than Ice Cream

Meaning ignites the will. All these people I was watching were doing what they were doing because they wanted to. Something had ignited their will. They could go on forever, or nearly so, doing what they were doing. They believed in it. There was something in it for them. It had meaning for them. But nothing had meaning for me. And so my will lay dormant, like a great brown bear in the dead of winter.

With a glance I surveyed all that mankind was doing and what people hoped to attain by it. It was all emptiness and foolishness, self-deception and slavery. Yes, they were busy, and yes, their wills were ignited and they were all aflame with achievement. But the meaning that was stirring them was illusory.

Fame could not keep back the ravages of age nor the final rendezvous with death. Building houses and spawning families and amassing millions affected nothing. All and everything had to be relinquished at the dark door. Time was going to have its way with us. We acted as if we were going to be here forever, and that there was no death, and no great cosmos beyond our petty, narrow strivings.

I was an outsider. I felt it in my bones like the ache of growing pains. I was outside of the meaning that stirred the society around me into action. Moreover, I saw that the meaning people believed in and valued and threw their lives away on was a lie. And it was a lie that could only exist if they were willing to ignore reality. It was a bubble of ignorance and vanity.

So what could I do? I saw the meaninglessness of what passed for meaning in everyday life. I knew I needed to find meaning if I was ever to make something of my life. Without meaning to arouse my will I was as good as dead.

But where would I find this elusive meaning? I didn't even have the fire to start searching for it.

So I sat down. I sat in my chair by the window overlooking the fire escape, the grimy alley and its bashed and tumbled garbage cans. I stared ahead, my shoulders hunched, like someone waiting on a wintry corner for a streetcar that may or may not come.

Now, it so happened one Sunday morning, as the shy and tentative spring was coaxing winter away, as I sat in my chair staring ahead, seeing double and bemoaning the fate that made me unable to read or go to the movies, an inspiration hit me. I turned on the radio, and there came into my ears a voice, a mellow, modulated, mellifluous voice intoning the King's English and speaking, of all things, philosophy. Not philosophy as I had known it in college — fuzzy and non-committal — but something clear and strong and full of promise.

Transfixed, I listened to each word the way I did in the hearing tests they used to give us in elementary school. This man was talking about my plight! He was talking about the need to know and understand the meaning of life! He had been working on the problem and he had found some-thing, something of great importance — the most important discovery since the Renaissance, he said. Sound had become light in my mind. The prom-ise of life rang in that voice. Who is he, who is he, who is he???

The announcement at the end of the talk gave me a shock and a new direction. The announcer said it was Pacifica Radio (which seemed so poi-gnant) and that the speaker with the beautiful En-glish voice was Colin Wilson (of whom I'd never heard) and that he had written a book called *The Outsider*.

Revived, I raced off to a bookstore and on the way stopped at my friend Mike's apartment. He read to a 90-year old lady for a living and he liked to read aloud and it wasn't hard to play on his sym-pathy about my encroaching blindness and per-suade him to read *The Outsider* to me aloud.

What I learned as I listened to Mike read the book was that I was in good company. Most of the men I admired were outsiders — Jesus and Buddha and Lawrence of Arabia and William Blake and Van Gogh — a cavalcade of stars and heroes. None of them believed in the values of the societies they found themselves in. They struggled, sometimes successfully and sometimes not, to find the truth, the real meaning of life. I was encouraged by the quality of this company and the heroism of their efforts.

You can't be outside of something without being inside of something else. As we neared the latter part of the book I felt a new stirring in me. I felt like an insider to the real, deeper meaning of life. Though I didn't know exactly what it was, like a spiritual hound dog I was getting the scent of something. I wanted to follow that scent. I was sure it would lead me to the real in the midst of the unreal.

A book is a dead thing and cannot satisfy a living hunger, even a brilliant book like *The Outsider*. I needed to find something real, something living. All the outsiders of the book were long dead. I needed to find a living, learning situation that was happening now, in New York. I needed to find a school.

And I wouldn't have known where to turn next had not Colin Wilson mentioned — at the very end of his book — a practical method of realizing truth that was currently being practiced, the legacy left by a great contemporary outsider and spiritual adventurer named Gurdjieff...

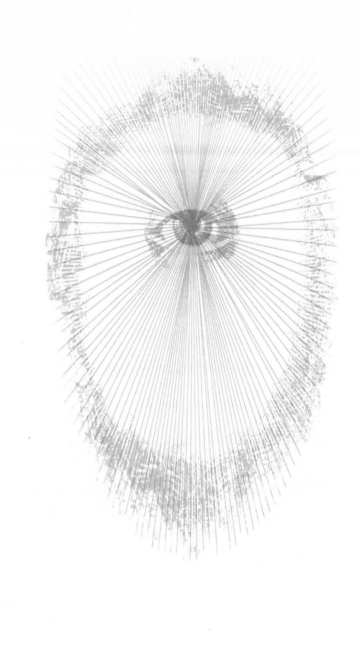

Taste the Sun

Sometimes I think my youth was misspent in a headlong living-out of the metaphors that I would need in later life to get across my message. So here we go: at the center of a lot of what we did on the streets and in the schoolyards was a pink ball called a Spaldeen, accent on the second syllable. A fresh, powdery, high-bouncing Spaldeen so lifted our hearts it was as if Life, out of its illimitable abundance, was giving us yet another second chance. With that bright ball sailing from hand to hand the day held promise and zest and unforeseen possibilities of glory.

When we bought a new Spaldeen, the first

thing we did was test it by slamming it down onto the sidewalk to see how high it would bounce. The sight of it against the baby-blue sky of Brooklyn enthralled us. It spoke to us too, in the heart-talk that images speak. Deep and stirring, it spoke of aspiration, striving from the lower levels to the higher ones and of achievement.

Now that's my metaphor! The secret of the Spaldeen's high bounce was the fullness and intensity of its contact with the earth — the same secret man needs to know in order to reach the heights he is capable of reaching. "Come down to earth!" was the way my father put it when I was hovering around the house in one of my collegiate fantasies. When we come to earth we make the contact that can send us up to another level, to another medium fertile with new and grander possibilities.

We are born to come to earth, floating in the womb-waters, struggling down the canal, finally gasping out into a chilly world. But from that moment, influences of every kind conspire to keep us from a deep, ultimate contact with the earth. These influences are so persistently pernicious that most of us never arrive. We actually never come to *be* here. We're never present on the earth, and therefore never make the connection that could propel us from this lovely, temporary place to another place, more lovely and more fitting, that awaits us.

Graciously, the means for this salutary connection are always spread out before us. Each day, many times a day, food appears on our plates. And we eat. This food we eat, in all its amazing variety, is it not the body of the earth? But to make that contact with the earth we have to do more than merely feed like animals. We humans are obliged to eat like humans. Our senses must be attuned to what we are doing. Most particularly, our taste buds must be awake to what we are eating, for it is through the portal of taste that we make the most intimate contact with the earth. All our glorious sciences, all religions, all our philosophies amount to nothing if we do not taste our food.

The human act of eating is meant to nourish our whole being — body, mind, and feelings. If we just mindlessly pop food into our mouths while we talk, dream or even read when we should be tasting, we treat ourselves like fuel-guzzling machines. But by connecting to our sense of taste, being there as we eat, tasting every morsel as we eat it, we feed our very essence, which is the source of all our possibilities.

It's not by accident that food has a taste, nor, that the memory of its taste moves us to eat that food again, nor that the savor of certain foods lingers on our palate long after the bill has been paid and forgotten. Taste draws us into meaningful contact with the earth. Taste transmits the meaning of food.

From the ordinary to the most profound levels, the way you know about food is by tasting it. Through tasting you know if you want it, if you like it, if it's good for you, if it's gone bad. At a deeper level, if the food gets by your palate unnoticed (due to haste, heedlessness or inattention) you've missed a crucial moment of knowing. Your palate is your sentry, your watchman, guarding what you are allowing into the most intimate chemistry of your body. Out of this chemical wedding arises the being of tomorrow.

Taste is the contact point that enables the ball to bounce high. By actually being present at the moment of tasting we are not merely exercising our capacity, we are refining it. Within our ordinary taste we are awakening to a higher taste. By tasting we come to realize how mere earthbound foods do not fully satisfy; then a hunger can arise in us for a finer food, a food from another level that can lift us up. The food of earth keeps us earthly; it keeps us mortal. The finer food sends us heavenward, making us immortal.

This finer food is everywhere about us, permeating everything on the earth. Shocked into increased presence by our new-found hunger, we will find that finer food. Its taste is the taste of the sun.

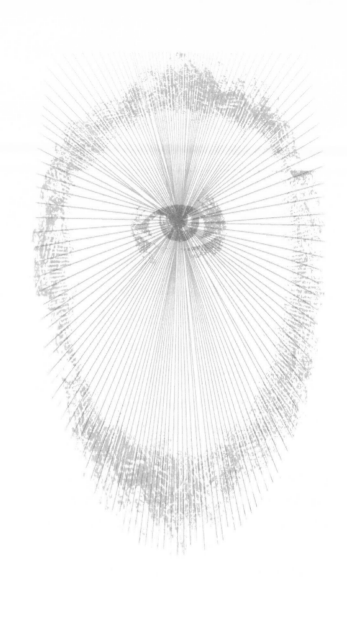

My Kind of Dog

Here's what he used to say, my father, when we asked him where he had been and what he had done:

He used to say: "I had to see a man about a dog."

Now as simple sentences go that's as good a simple sentence as I've ever heard. And since simple sentences are designed to convey something — a complete thought — my father's sentence neither conveyed what it was apparently conveying nor could it in any way be thought to be a thought, let alone a complete thought. It was a sentence that was intended to say something beyond any of its words or its apparent syntax.

And because it spoke so many volumes, I have pondered its possible meanings over many long years.

Here's my harvest of what I found in it:

1. Don't ask me because I'm not going to tell you.

2. Where I go and what I do is my business, not yours.

3. I did go out and I had to go out, that I will admit.

4. Whenever I do go out my business is always about one thing or another and it may have been about this.

5. The reasons I go out are all of equal importance.

6. All that I might say and do is symbolism, always symbolism.

7. None of the reasons I go out could be better expressed than in this way.

8. Regardless of when I go out and what I do when I am out, there will always be a

dog and there will always be a man.

9. And there will be a relationship between the man and the dog.

10. What the man has to say about the dog may be of some significance, equaled only by what the dog leaves unsaid about the man.

11. But who is or was the man? And who was the dog?

12. And why is this all so seemingly significant, about dogs and men?

And lastly,

13. Why didn't my father just tell me what he meant instead of causing me to spend my life figuring it out?

All of this is neither here nor there, except the matter of the relationship of man to dog and dog to man. In this, the New Age, where there's so much talk of "relationships" or "conscious relating" it's always about human to human. That's good as far as it goes. But I want to tell you what I've seen in a dog's eyes.

There are as many kinds of dogs as there are humans. And they are all at different levels. So there are dogs that are real lowdown dogs — dogs that like to go around pretending they're just dopey four-legged tail-waggers, tongues hanging out, ready to snap at a passing fly to prove their hot doggery, and there are dogs that nip at our heels (symbolically, of course).

This heel-nipping kind of dog is the kind of dog I want to tell you about. I know this kind of dog.

I have this kind of dog. Actually, she's not my dog. This is my wife's dog. She's a Schnauzer — the dog, that is, a Schnauzer of medium size; salt and pepper. Get the picture?

Now I've looked into this dog's eyes, and she looks back into mine. She looks at me with that look. She's so intelligent; she's so knowing; and she looks out from her heart.

Not every kind of dog has that knack. They may be working their way to that kind of look, but they don't all have it yet.

This dog is top of the line, you might say. Top of the heap. She's looking out from across a gulf. She's saying something from behind those deep, brown eyes. And those eyes are saying what it is fortunate her tongue can't say, because we would laugh at her if she could. I mean, we humans.

She's saying: I'm waiting for you. She's not talking about waiting to go outside and do dog business. She's waiting for something else. But what, you may ask? If only she could answer; if only she could speak.

She tries. She tries to speak. She has a range of expression that reaches its highest form when my wife has been away for too long a time. The sound is so full of the ache of missing a person, the agony of being without my wife's presence, and the re-criminations that go with it. She nearly breaks into an operatic aria.

What she means when her eyes say that she is waiting for you is — now, you're not going to believe this, I know. You'll think I'm fooling. Or being fanciful. What I'm going to tell you is too true, that's why you're not going to believe me.

And it's going to be too close to the bone, and you're not going to like it. That's why you're not going to believe what I'm going to tell you. But I'm going to tell you anyway.

This dog is waiting to become a human being.

That's right. She wants to step into the form of a human. Don't ask me why, considering the pathetic figure most of us humans cut. Maybe she thinks she can do it better, although I don't think she's a competitive creature. I think she recognizes there's a lot more possibilities when you step into the human skin.

I suppose all the animals, in one way or another, are waiting for the same thing. Because it's a pretty great opportunity, this business of being human, though most of us don't take advantage of it. We take advantage of most everything else — other humans, the earth, God and all His spiraling nebulae. You might say that's our foremost characteristic — we take advantage. Yet we don't seem to be able to take advantage of our golden opportunity.

This dog wants that opportunity. She'd make a great human being, too. She's got a lot of the qualities that we're supposed to have. She's quick to size up a situation; she sees through people's facades; she's not afraid — I've seen her go up to dogs five times her size. She's gentle, considerate, unassuming, unprepossessing, patient, long-suffering, always ready for new adventures, dependable, reliable, sympathetic, level-headed, level-hearted in bright times and dark. She's loyal to a fault, hope pours from her heart like a fountain, she mourns for those she loves, she knows how to wait, never looks for and therefore never finds fault. She respects things. Every step she takes is princess-like, dainty and full of attention.

I could go on. But you understand that with those qualities alone she has a head start. She can become anything she wants. Most of all, she can *become*. Unlike those of us humans who have made complacency a fine art, she knows — I know she knows — that to take on the human form is the longing of the whole animal kingdom, and she is prepared to assume the privilege as well as the obligation.

This dog, given half a chance, could become a human that the race would be proud of. She could go all the way. She could serve the highest good. Steadfastly, too. She could become transformed. After all, dog is you-know-what spelled backwards.

Sometimes, you have to see a dog about a man.

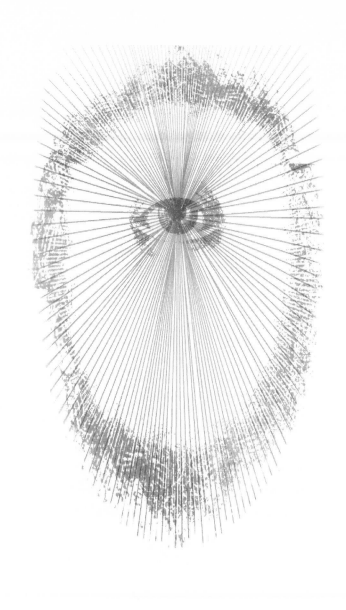

Traveling is the Way to Go

I started out with the right idea. I suppose we always do. But before long I went astray. And I'm still trying to get back.

Back then, when I knew what things were about, I didn't use the words "traveling" or "journeying." The simple words that sent a thrill through me were "We're going to go somewhere." These magic words were usually spoken by my father, and backed up by my mother, who usually urged me to drop what I was doing and get dressed or they were going to leave without me. She never had to tell me a second time, and they never left without me.

INSIGHT IS BETTER THAN ICE CREAM

The news that we were going out somewhere always came out of the blue. I was never there for the planning. In the world I grew up in, adults didn't plan outings based on my, or any child's, whim. My parents decided where they wanted to go or who they wanted to visit and we — my sister, my brother and I — went with them. We were a family, after all.

The smell of my father's Pontiac held its new-car freshness long after other men's cars were rusting in junkyards. He kept it in mothballs in the garage and only took it out on Sundays and special occasions. We tumbled in, we three in our finery, Rina and Dennis and I, all in the back seat. My father always drove, wearing his fedora and dark blue coat and chewing Chiclets, which he always chewed when we went out and which he distributed equally to all passengers. My mother sat beside him in her magenta hat with a veil on it and her shiny Persian lamb coat and high heels. That was the finishing touch, my mother in high heels. That signaled we were going some place important. Usually Staten Island.

That's where we went mostly. At least that's what I remember most. That's where I had been born, and that's where all my aunts and uncles, my father's brothers and sisters, lived and that was where my wild cousins were and, of course, the most important man in the world, Don Cicce, my grandfather.

His nickname was "La Scell Du Roof" which means, in his native Barese dialect, "The Ladder That Goes to the Roof." He was a tall man, and he had a towering ego. He was the kind of man you wanted to meet and dreaded to meet at the same time.

That was our usual destination — Staten Island, the relatives and my grandfather, Il Gran Signor, Franceesk Antonio Croceet. (I'm spelling it like it sounded, but you also have to roll the r's to get the right flavor.)

In order to get there in those days we had to

take the ferry. We waited on a line that sometimes wound all the way up to Owl's Head Park, where we could look out at the moody waters of The Narrows and further, to the green, promising hills of Staten Island.

Once we got on the ferry, which usually took a goodly chunk of forever, we all popped out of the Pontiac like seeds out of a seedpod and scattered over the boat. I ran over to the side — running was what I mostly did in those days — so I could see the water, up close, face-to-face, green and blue and black and bubbly and white with foam and rainbowed with oil and scraps of wood and seagulls floating, the rich wide world of the water of The Narrows, a part of New York harbor that connected to the vast Atlantic and all the seas of the world. What a wonder it was!

That's why we had come out, that's why I'd dropped everything, got ready, dressed up and suffered so long waiting in line, so I could ride the water and be nose to nose with it and look into its depths and inhale its sweet-and-sour smells. This was something worth going out for. We lived only a few blocks from The Narrows and I walked to it and rode my bike to it innumerable times. I could always see it from shore.

But it was different to be on it, to be held up by it, to be intimate with it, to be at its mercy. I loved the sea; it drew me down to the heart of its mystery. Where we were headed, our destination, didn't matter. All the rigmarole of visiting that would take us late into the night, so late that I would invariably sleep on the journey back, meant nothing compared to this time on the water, riding the snarling white-caps on the fat, matronly, steel-plated Staten Island Ferry.

I knew that, then. All the destinations that we have and strive to get to and scurry to be on time for mean nothing, however much they are touted and advertised. The wonders are to be found on the way *to* those places; what really matters and is worth seeing and experiencing happens on the way to those destinations. Maybe we have to concoct an itinerary and set a destination in order to find what's worth seeing on the way. I think we forget, as we get older, about what's really worth seeing; we get sucked into believing that the destination is all that matters and that travelling is about getting to a place.

I knew it when I was a boy. I got caught up when I got older. The rush and scramble to get to places and see the sights overwhelmed me as I got older. I've actually spent my fortune and exhausted myself to see old, broken down castles and big erector sets like the Eiffel Tower and statues and memorials and mountains, although I could always hear Henry David whispering over my shoulder:

"I have traveled much in Concord."

I know what he means now. I think I always knew, but I've been hustled along by my self and my dreams and by other people and their timetables. There's a way of traveling that allows a person to see what really is worth seeing and to know that thereby one is feeding one's soul. You have to be alert and be able to stop and stay with what is beckoning to you.

Now, after travelling around the world a time or two I see that all my destinations have left me empty. But on the way there were wild, wonderful things and places that beckoned to me and fed me. There was a place in Turkey where wild oregano was growing and the wind was softly swirling the fragrance of the flowers. There was a stairway down a cliff leading to the leper colony in Molokai and guava fruit made the air soft and wild with longing. I passed through a gypsy camp behind the Alhambra and I remember the children's big, dark lustrous eyes. A breakfast place in Persia where there was a white, self-possessed donkey grazing by the road; his mouth made most musical chewing. A moonlit night on the Big Sur that was so magical I sat on the grass half the night. And some Christmas lights I saw in a hilltown in Italy; a vision of paradise in a dark world.

These little places that feed the soul are everywhere. You don't have to go far. Just step out your door. Just the other day I noticed the juniper tree outside my window. It drew me outside. I looked at it a long time. One could go around the world, seeing all the usual sights and never see such a tree. Or touch such a tree. Or hug it, knowing you've found a friend.

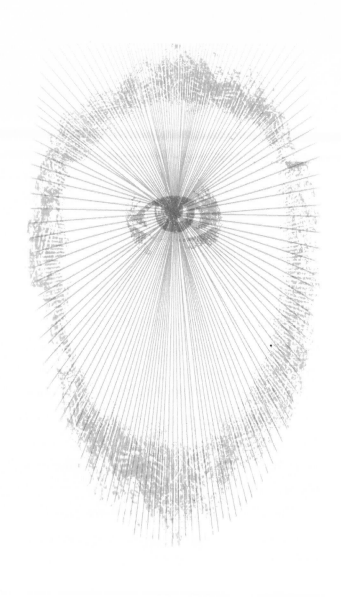

To the Health of
Dr. Frank Rathbone

I knew him. Long ago, before there were Ziploc bags and a hole in the sky; and faraway, where money talked but not everyone listened, where the ballpark was small and real enough so that every so often a ghost-white ball would go over the fence, bouncing with superb, unpredictable innocence into traffic on Bedford Avenue, where a ferry took you to an island off the coast of North America for a mere nickel. I knew him when he was an unassuming, untrumpeted, member of the faculty.

The school, Brooklyn College, was broad and bosomy, sprawling languorously under the Flatbush sun. They called it a subway college, to diminish its stature even further, for you could live at home and ride the subway there. It was an extension of the same crummy public educational system that was a prerequisite for entry. Nothing was going to happen, nothing was going to be learned (certainly nothing relevant) and after four years within its bland and benign walls great numbers of inmates were released amid much fanfare and speechifying.

When you're not expecting anything is the best time to be hit with the unexpected. So, unsuspecting, we freshmen sulked our way across the quad, across Avenue H to the Pfizz Ed Building where we flopped noisily into seats and defied anyone to teach us anything about Health Ed. That was the course — Health Ed. A preposterous required course. The name printed in the instructor box was "RATHBONE."

That first day, we slouched into some semblance of comfort and prepared to sleep. We waited with increased irritation as the clock ticked a full

ten minutes past the hour, until a loudmouth began to trouble the rabble with declarations that
we didn't have to wait more than ten minutes for
an instructor to appear and who the hell was he to
be late on the first day and let's all get out of this
dump and maybe we should leave this Rathbone
a note.

Then in he came.

Then in *he* came. Strolling, mind you. As if
he were unaware or unconcerned or perhaps glad
to be late. He paid no attention to us and our irritation, went to his desk, which had neither
books nor papers on it, went to the window as if
checking on the growth of the mountain laurel
blossoming outside and then, with the thought-
fulness a man might experience sitting alone in
his own parlor pondering a problem he was having with his septic system, he went to his chair,
leaned back and carefully placed his sneakered feet
up on the desk.

They were white sneakers. He had dark ath-

letic-looking pants with a silvery-grey stripe up
the sides, and a grey flannel polo shirt. He looked
a little like Dick Tracy, but with a larger, more
determined jaw. His eyes were dark brown and
marvelously alert. He carried his large, gleaming
bald head proudly, as if it covered some meaningful gray matter. Had he had wings and some pierc-
ing, patriotic concerns he might have posed for
any number of dollar bills. He was the unexpected.

Frank Rathbone — *Doctor* Frank Rathbone
had come to teach Health Ed. As he understood
the subject, it encompassed everything. How can
a person be healthy if he doesn't know about the
nature and ultimate purpose of the universe, about
God and his inscrutable ways, about what the earth
is and its place in the great harmony, what life is,
what human beings are and their function in the
universal scheme, how to properly relate to other
humans, what sex is all about, how to know yourself, what possible use a college education is, what
greatness in a man consists of, the uses or misuses

of the past, what is death, what is its relation to life, how to maintain a bodily state that can serve a person to develop innate but unmanifest powers, what is the mind, how can it be used to good purpose...

Oh, Rathbone took us for a ride. We discussed everything. And talking with him was worlds away from the kind of talk we did in other classes. You had to think; you couldn't get away with blather. And his presence was an example. If you asked him a question, he'd think! There was nothing pre-cooked about the man. He taught us to think — and think freshly. I had never seen it before and I haven't seen it since.

Though he never mentioned him I suspect the good Doctor was a follower of Pythagoras. To know and to understand and to be was the way to Health. Real health is the health of the being, the whole being, not merely the health of the body. He saw the desperate striving for mere physical fitness alone to be the futile efforts of ignorant men and women. To attain that perfect balance in all three worlds one must place oneself under the star of Hygeia, the five-pointed star of Pythagoras.

I don't know where Dr. Frank Rathbone is now. Regretably I lost sight of him, lost touch with him. But wherever he is — on the earth or beyond it — may this lifting of glasses by me and my friends find him in the best of health and (since he never stopped striving) ever getting better. I drink, then, to the health of Doctor Frank Rathbone!

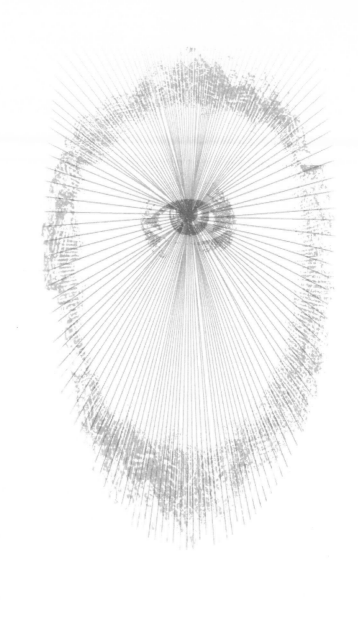

How to Die Before You Die

It was high noon. The perfect time. He was a little boy, the finest among us. He tapped me and said, matter-of-factly: "Bang. You're dead." Words beyond words. Words of ultimate power.

I turned, swiftly, shocked. No one expects to be erased in a supermarket parking lot, bang, suddenly, without apparent reason.

There he was. There were his eyes. The eyes of this diminutive manslayer looked like bullet tips. Blank and blue. His blond hair encircled his angelic face like a heavenly insignia. His skin was pure, his teeth were white. He wore a polo shirt, designer jeans and sneakers that had blue wings at the heels.

And in his hand he held a golden gun trained

impertinently at my heart, at my still-beating heart.

Had I not, just then, come from a difference of opinion with a young lady with rings in her ears, nose and tongue who was supposedly staffing the supposed express check-out and who insisted — in her breathy, sing-song Valley Girl blah-zay — that it didn't matter if "redripetomatoes" went to the bottom of a bag and two monstrous torpedo-size cans of pineapple juice went on top, I might have been amused by the Lilliputian bushwacker before me.

I glared at him. I glared a long time. I sneered, slowly. He never wavered. He never quailed. He never flinched. After a long while, a slow, cold smile slid across his lips like a contemptuous serpent.

He was three or four. I'm older. A lot older. So, even though he'd gotten the drop on me, the showdown seemed a bit unequal. I relented. I smiled back, with a little warmth.

I said, "Is that how you say hello?"

He shuffled and shrugged. Then he gave me a real smile.

"How do you like my gun?" he asked, offering the gun for my inspection.

'Twas a fine gun, it was, too. Real metal, with a revolving barrel and pure white handles, made of something that wasn't pearl but wasn't plastic either, and it shone like the soul of childhood, for it was very, very gold.

Holding that gun out there in the sunlight of the parking lot, my mind drifted back to a time when I thought of nothing but pulling the trigger and proclaiming that Louie or Paulie or Jimmy or Vince was dead — all of them my friends, my dearest and best friends. Of course, then, they had the presence of mind to contradict me.

"You missed!!!"

And "Bang!" I was dead.

That's how it went when we were kids; we were killing each other off all the time. We took death as part of a game, a great part. We fell over and writhed, gasped and died. We loved to play the death scene. We died magnificently.

Sometimes we died and came back. We'd leap back into life again, claiming we had never been dead at all. In those fresh, daring days we didn't take any of it seriously. We laughed in the face of death. We had so much life in us death was a joke with egg on its face. Just another fantasy.

Later, having grown up and swallowed Adam's apple, death became a serious matter, nothing to sneeze at, the one fly in the ointment of life, a bitter, inexorable pill we all had to take, a *fact* — not a fantasy — a fact to be dreaded and dodged. No one could stave it off, not Gandhi, not Sinatra, not Gurdjieff. It became the ultimate shadow, waiting patiently, like the long face of the undertaker.

"Great gun you've got," I said, and pulled the trigger. Point blank.

He stumbled back against a post, slid down it and went limp as pudding. He groaned a heartrending groan. He spasmed when he reached the macadam, rolled over. His left foot twitched at the end.

An old lady with purple hair passed and looked me over.

I was waiting for something to happen, the smoking gun in my hand.

An eternity passed like the flap of an eagle's wing.

Then he opened his eyes, squinting, as if to make sure I was still there — there on the hard pitch of the parking lot under a pitiless sun. I reassured him I wasn't there. For he was dead. Through-and-through dead. That was it. I squatted down and tried to get my point across. But he would have none of it. He was in a state of denial. To prove his point he struggled to his feet. I battered him with facts: there was the gun, there was the bullet, it was point blank range, the bullet went through his chest and out the other side, he had felt it, he had groaned, he had fallen.

INSIGHT IS BETTER THAN ICE CREAM

He only laughed and yanked the gun out of my hand and ran off, shouting that he'd been "only making believe!" He raced heedlessly across the parking lot, his blond curls bouncing, towards where his mother was waiting with open arms.

I lifted my long-range rifle, the black one with the scope on it and Ping! I got him in the back, beautifully. But he kept on going.

The kid was indestructible.

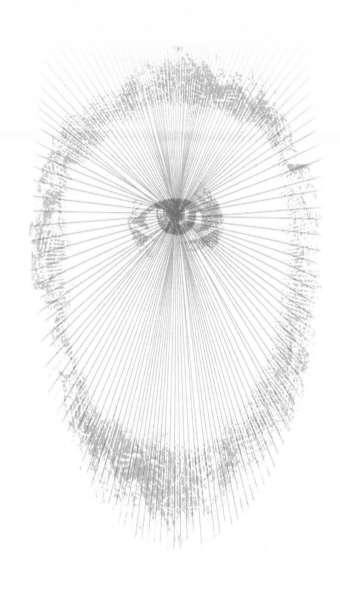

Found Money

Ah, Cynthia was sweet,
her lips, her thighs,
her succulent feet.

Revenge, too, and worldly success,
though vile and vain,
bring sweetness nonetheless.

Yet sweeter even than goldenrod honey,
sweeter than high summer,
is money, money, found money.

Suddenly, without warning, when you least expect it, that's how fortune strikes, good or bad.

Insight is Better Than Ice Cream

So it was on that Indian Summer day long ago. I was hardly ready.

The day, the year, all that scaffolding we make so much of, eludes me. I was there, I remember that. And the day was one of those days that drives yellow jackets and young boys wild, sending them to search out the last drops of nectar before the heart-chill of winter sets in. We had our skates out and we were all over the street.

The year had an invisible structure consisting of a succession of appropriate activities — sledding and snowballing and ice-skating and handball and punchball and bows-and-arrows and swords and carpet-guns and soap-box scooters and football and skates and hockey and waterguns and playing-cards and stoop-ball and bicycles and marbles. No one told us when to do what. When the time came we knew and we submitted delightedly to the next wave. This time, the time that I speak of, was the time for skates.

Our skates were primitive. They were strapped onto our shoes, and they had metal grippers that were tightened with a skate key. The length and the width of the skates were adjustable. The wheels were metal which through constant wear lost their roundness and became "boxed wheels," a dreaded phenomenon. All in all those skates served us well.

Since it was morning and the last day we would have to skate, we didn't need a game to keep us interested. Skating for the love of skating was enough. The 20 or 30 kids who were out under the sun were engaged in untrammeled, unsupervised wildness — dashing and looping and crisscrossing, skinning one another, bumping or circling, skidding to sudden stops, leaping the curbs, racing and chasing. It was mayhem, very pure and very beautiful.

I was there as part of it all, weaving my wayward thread into the morning's tapestry. Graceful, daring, always testing and defying the edge of the parapet of impossibility. The thing I most hated was falling, not merely out of pride but mostly because it hurt my bones; I was very skinny.

What the adults of the world were doing never

occurred to us, except when a car passed, but that was rare. The street was our playground. Our parents sent us out and then went about their business. When a car appeared we parted to let it through and booed and stuck out our tongues as it passed. We owned the streets.

And so it was on that particular day, as I was skating with mad, blurry abandon, that I fell. Rather perfectly, right on my rump. It hurt. Other kids buzzed by me, razzing and heckling me. Trying to hide how much it hurt, I casually reached under my bottom and started to get up. I felt something beneath me. I looked and there, looking right up at me, was a twenty dollar bill.

I sat for a moment in a profound stillness. The movement and the shouting around me seemed very far away. A twenty! Unquestionably a twenty! And very, very green. The sounds and the skating all surged back.

I knew I had to think quickly. I glanced around. No one had seen it. I had my hand on it. How could it have been out here in the middle of the street all the while? Perhaps one of my friends had dropped it — impossible. No kid I knew had that kind of money. Pennies and nickels yes, and sometimes a dime. Sometimes we'd pool our coins together and get Tom the grocer to exchange it for a dollar or two so we could buy a pizza. That's the only time we touched green paper. None of my friends could have dropped this. And I'm not asking anyway. This is mine. This is my money. I found it, and finders keepers.

Bobby Gerson came gliding over to me. I ignored him. He's the one who handled the money whenever we bought pizza or anything else. He knew more about money then anyone else. He held out his hand. I pretended I didn't see it. He asked if I was okay.

"I'll help you up."

As I gave him my right hand I slipped the bill into my pocket with the left, feeling shrewd as a magician. He said I looked white. I said I was all right. I never said another word as I skated out of the whirligig of skaters and blazed down the block toward my house.

The sun, the mild, sweet weather and the twenty blended into a ball of ecstasy. I was in the middle of that ball; that ball was in the middle of me. Though I was flailing my arms and pushing off as hard as I could the ride to my house was a slow, intolerable journey, during which I began to worry that my twenty wasn't safe in my pocket. It might slip out. Stranger, more perverse things have happened. I checked and it was still in my pocket, but I knew it could only be safe if I had it in my hand, and not just any hand but my right hand. So as I was coasting down the block (our block had a nice slope to it) I took the bill out of my pocket with my left hand and transferred it to my right. When it was in my left hand I could hardly feel it so I clutched it very tightly in my right. Now, I had it. And it couldn't get away from me.

Obstacles and threats loomed the closer I got to home. Somebody called my name. I think it was Mr. Silvestri in his rose garden, and he called out something in Italian. On the left side of the street Fat Richie was sponging his sleek black De Soto. He made a feint toward me as if he was going to grab me, and he flung some soapy water out of his big fat sponge. Most of it missed me but a little got into my left eye. I determined that if I were going to fall I would hold that money tighter than a Gila Monster and roll over and hold my arm close to me. Blinking fast helped but it's amazing how long it takes for soap to stop burning your eyes. Then, just then, as I was only a few houses away from home, Jack De Presca decides to back his green Packard out of his alleyway. He moves it like he's navigating the Queen Mary, slow and stately ...

Then I was there, swinging into my own driveway. All the way home I'd been framing the right words. As I raced down the street, the wind parting back my hair, jumping over the manhole covers and the gaps and the cracks in the tar and occasional splats of car oil, I rehearsed possible ways of announcing my triumph. Now, rattling onto the concrete of the alleyway my mouth said what it wanted to and my voice echoed against the walls of the house.

"Ma! Ma! Dad!"

When I whirled round the back of the house my mom and dad were emerging from the cellar, their faces shadowed with worry and dread. Usually I called that urgently because I was bleeding. But I was all smiles this time, holding out my twenty like it was the pearl of great price. Relieved, they gathered around me, smiling too.

"Look! Look what I found!"

With both my parents around me, my happiness and glory were complete. It seemed the universe was on my side. Rarely were both my mother and father in the same place at the same time. My father was usually fixing something or printing wedding invitations on his great thumping press or leaving for work or sleeping before leaving for work since he worked the night shift while my mother was washing floors or making lunch or sewing curtains. This triumphant morning they had been both in the basement helping my grandparents stuff a year's worth of tomato sauce into Ball jars.

We were a happy tableau for some few moments. Then my mother began to quiz me. When she was satisfied that the money wasn't ill-gotten she told me to go back and play. In that moment I realized that it wasn't enough to have and hold this fortune in my hand. I had to do something with it then if it was eventually to be translated into the means of satisfying my desires. And in that same moment my mother saw my quandary. She took the twenty out of my hand.

"We'll put it in the bank for you," she said.

My father agreed. "Good idea."

"For safe keeping," she said.

I protested. I hadn't raced down the block, nearly killing myself, to bury my money in some bank. I wailed. I had plans for that beautiful twenty dollar bill. My chest began to sob and my eyes watered. They tried to "reason" with me, but when they saw how little interest I had in it, they went back to canning tomatoes, leaving me on my skates under the indifferent Indian Summer sun, surrounded by bushels of ripe, red, unsympathetic tomatoes.

That was the last I saw of that wondrous twenty dollar bill. Where it went I am not sure. Maybe it really did go into a bank account. More likely it went into the flow of money that kept my family alive and well in those happy but not-very-affluent years.

But where that *actual* twenty dollar bill is now I would really like to know. Perhaps it's in the billfold of someone in California or on the other side of the world. Perhaps it got worn out and wallet-weary and was taken out of circulation …

I had such plans for that money. I wanted my friends to know I had such a mighty resource. I wanted to buy pizzas, and a cap gun and a red shirt with criss-cross laces like the Lone Ranger and a baseball hat and a magic set and a microscope and a telescope like pirates used and a globe that spins and a gyroscope and at least one pair of socks that weren't *Irregular.*

"You'll have something for a rainy day," my father had said.

Ah, but who cares about rainy days when the sun is shining? And I continued to think such thoughts in the deep desolation of my childhood soul. I took off my skates and wandered to the front of the house, where I sat on the stoop for a long time.

It seemed to me I had lost everything. Not just the money. I had lost all my possibilities. And all the things I had dreamt of. I had lost all my enthusiasm for skating, for Indian Summer, for the hockey game that we were probably going to play later on. I realized I'd lost my appetite for living. I'd lost my life …

Of course I was only a kid, about 11 or so and I couldn't think my way out of the jungle I was in. I knew, though, that something had fooled me or perhaps tricked me. Somehow I had put all my hopes in that green piece of paper till nothing else mattered. It became more important than my friends and the air and the sun and even my own life. And it had happened so fast. I sat there in the vague, lifeless hope that this would all pass and I would come back to life again. After a while, though my heart still hung heavy as a stone, I put my skates back on and made my way back up the block.

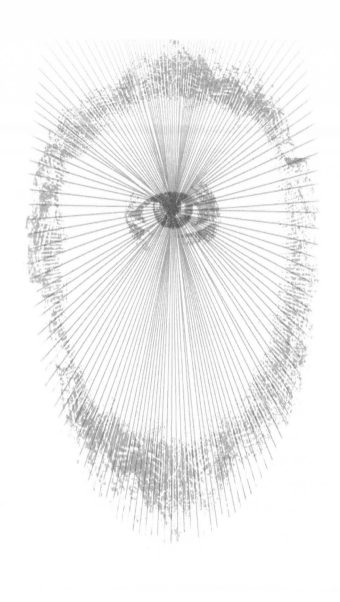

Come Unity

The string breaks, the beads scatter: a breath-taking return to chaos. With a sigh the lady kneels on the linoleum and methodically picks up one slippery bead at a time, all the while refusing to be overwhelmed by the immensity and seeming hopelessness of the task.

They have found their way behind the legs of chairs, under the stove, against the baseboard, in the far corner, under the counter, by the saddle between the kitchen and the dining room, in the dining room under the breakfront; two even make it into the plush blue carpeting of the living room. The latent mischievousness of beads shows itself when they get loose. Eventually the lady's persistent fingers pluck them up, every last one, drop them in a bowl ready for re-stringing, a return to the unity of the circular necklace.

Sometimes it takes a long time for those loose beads to be found. While they wait for the graceful fingers to re-gather them, they undergo the agony that comes with separation from the circle of unity, the *community* of beads.

I have felt the ache of separation since I was a boy. It is written on my face in all family photographs of me. I look out, a little skinny fellow, from across a great gulf. Close as we were in the family, we were so far apart.

Even on the block, the team games we played — punch-ball and stickball and slap-ball — were brief, uneasy attempts at a unified effort, for things were always teetering on the edge of disintegration. Later, in college play productions and community theatre and then off-Broadway, the moments of working together were painfully rare. Separate, at odds, drowning in disunity was the way it went.

Though the same lack of community — many working and being as one — was evident in the religion I was baptized into, I did encounter something there that stirred me, inspired me and gave me an aim that has filled my little life. This something came in the form of a book, a little black book edged reddish-gold gilt, with red, raised letters on its cover that said *My Daily Psalm Book* against a picture of a great golden harp over a radiant earth.

I don't know how it came into my hands, but when I got it I held it tight. It was an intimate little book, the kind you carry in your pocket and feel its warmth, and the more you use it the warmer it gets. I used it. Most of the one hundred and fifty psalms are rich and beautiful and they get more beautiful with each praying. Through them I came to understand Jesus better; he prayed the psalms throughout his life and their rich profundity permeated his way of looking at things.

What made the book even more precious

were the pictures in it. They were pen and ink drawings, done with astonishing skill and imagination, exuding such heartfelt sincerity that often looking at the picture beside the psalm was enough to open your heart to the praying you were about to do.

The title page credited the drawings to one Ariel Agemian. The name meant nothing to me; it seemed Armenian, and Ariel might be a man or a woman. The drawings moved me deeply and I showed them to everyone. In those youthful days I did not try to contain my enthusiasms.

So it happened that as my enthusiasms were bending the long-suffering ears of my friend, Frank Tripoli, I showed him the drawings in the psalm-book. He looked at them appreciatively. Then he looked at me and laughed and said, "I know this guy."

So it came to pass that on the morning of October 30, 1956 I went to see Ariel Agemian. The day had a nip to it, so we decided not to walk but go in Frank's temperamental jalopy. The house we were bound for was on one of those bay streets that dead end at the Belt Parkway. (The Belt is Brooklyn's busy, whizzy highway that follows the harbor and then The Narrows, and after skirting Coney Island, heads past the beaches and marshes and mountains of landfill out toward the greatest dead end of all — LoneGuyLand.) I don't remember the number of the street but they look pretty much the same down that way. Brick houses, attached, with wrought-iron gates and nothing to recommend them.

Mrs. Agemian greeted us at the door. She was still in her nightgown, with curlers in her hair — the standard uniform of a Brooklyn housewife. After warmly embracing Frank she led us to the basement where her husband had his studio.

"Ariel," she screeched, "two handsome young fellers to see you! Ariel, what are you, dead? Get up!"

Ariel had his back to us, bent over his drawing

board, obviously putting careful finishing touches on an unseen work. He turned his head slowly.

"There he is," she said. "What an ugly face he has. I don't know why but only ugly men were ever interested in me."

She laughed all the way upstairs.

As he walked over to us he said, "She has a lotta good qualities, my wife, but she doesn't show them right away."

"How long does it take?" Frank joked.

"Well, let me see," said Agemian, "we've been married almost forty-five years … last week she did something nice."

He smiled and snapped his tongue from cheek to cheek.

He was a short man, with a neatly domed bald head, bearded, in his sixties, bit of a belly, white undershirt, hairy arms, black pants, patent leather slippers. Not the artist I expected.

"This is my friend, Ariel — Frank."

"Ahh," he sang, "two Frankfurters!"

144

That's how our time with Ariel Agemian began. He invited us deeper into his studio, served us espresso and showed us his latest drawings. They surprised me by their largeness and by their superabundant detail. He was clearly a patient, painstaking man. The work had a flaring radiance that didn't fully transfer to the reduced size in the psalm-book.

He had put aside his work for the morning. He wanted to know about us. He wanted to know about me and about my interest in the psalms. He spoke of how he had hopes of stirring people's hearts by his drawings, for he thought people's hearts had grown cold. He said I was the first person that had ever come to see him and his drawings. I said I couldn't believe that.

"People have come to buy drawings and to do business," he countered, "but you came because you were moved. That's different. When the heart is moved, that's different. You have made me happy."

He went on and talked for most of the morning. He talked about Armenia, the country he had come from and the life there that had been destroyed by war. He spoke of the Armenian Massacres and the famine and the beauty of the songs they used to sing.

"Mostly sad songs," he said dreamily. "Why is it beauty and sadness so often go together?"

Suddenly, as if he awakened from a reverie, he asked if I had my psalm-book with me. I did, and I handed it to him. He riffled through it.

"The pictures are a little small," he said wistfully. "You know I did a drawing for every single psalm. One hundred and fifty. That's a lotta drawing. It took me three years. And Father Frey, the editor, said this was the first time it was ever done — a drawing for each psalm. Since the beginning of time. This is an important thing. And it all happened in this little basement."

He had an impish twinkle in his eye, and he moved his tongue from one cheek to another.

Then, pinning his gaze on me, he asked "Which one do you like best?"

"Of the drawings...?"

"No, I wouldn't put you on the spot like that. What *psalm* do you like best?"

It's nice to know the answer to a question without having to think about it.

"Number one thirty-two," I said.

"Ahhh," he responded significantly, "that's *the one*. That's the most important one in the whole batch."

Then he leaned back and looked out the little basement window where you could see crew-cut green grass and a rose bush still tumbling with red roses.

"Behold how good," he began, "and how pleasant it is for brethren to dwell in unity ..."

He watched as some rose petals loosened by the fitful October wind fell sadly and beautifully to the ground.

"King David must have had a glimpse of

heaven when he wrote that psalm. 'To dwell together in unity'…"

He turned quickly in his mahogany swivel chair, becoming the imp again. "And do you know what it's like? It's … 'like the precious oil upon the head, that ran down upon the beard, the beard of Aaron, that ran down to the edge of his robe.' That's what it's like!" And he laughed and when he did his belly quivered.

"Do you think that it's possible? On this earth? Mr. Frank whatever-your-name is?"

"Crocitto."

"Mr. Frank Crocitto!"

He pronounced my name like an affectionate challenge.

"I hope so," I said.

"I hope so too," he said.

After that the talk went to one thing and another: to Frank's mother, whom Agemian was very fond of, to his preference for roses, to what we were going to do when we got out of school.

148

All the while he held my little psalm-book in his hand.

And when the time came to go he wrote my name in the book and he wrote his name beside it. I still have the book.

Psalm 132

Behold how good and how pleasant it is,
for brethren to dwell together in unity:
Like the precious oil upon the head,
that ran down upon the beard,
The beard of Aaron, that ran down
to the edge of his robe;
It is as if dew like the dew of Hermon
were falling upon Mount Sion:
For there the Lord bestows blessing,
life forevermore.

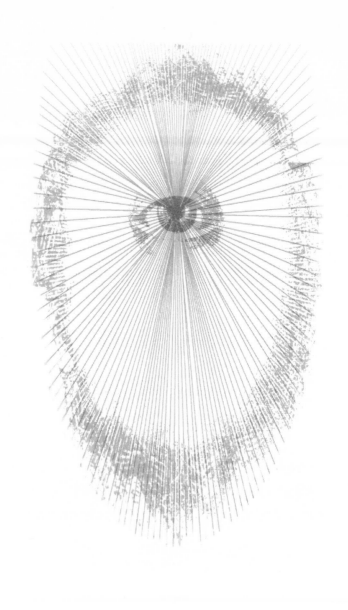

The Best Man

I met him when I first came up to the Valley
some thirty years ago. A tall, handsome man with
hair the color of cedar shakes before the weather
wears them gray. A strong boneyness to the face,
eyes hazel-green, kept in a squint as if he was having difficulty making out print on a page, and an
open, disarming smile that showed a lot of ivory.
When he walked he sauntered, as if he was loosely
pasted together, as if he had never found anything
worth hurrying for.

I give you all this description because it's of
no matter. He could have looked like any old body
around. He could have looked like you or me. His
looks were the least notable thing about him. The

way he did things, that's what counts, and what he showed of what was going on inside him, in the inner closet, you might say, where no one can go except the person himself. It's where all the valuables are kept, where the first stirrings of action take place, the place where, as we off-handedly say, the person is coming from.

He was coming out of the woods when I first met him dusting off a puffball mushroom big as a soccer ball. With the simple ease of someone who knows where he's come from, knows where he's going and knows what he's doing, he tossed it across the little clearing at me. Coming from the Big Apple I didn't know from mushrooms except to *beware*, they could be deadly poisonous, even to the touch. The Indians themselves, the "Native Americans," (though they may or may not have been native, and they were certainly not Americans) were scared to death of the things.

I caught it. Maybe that's why he stopped to chat. He didn't have much interest in cowardice.

He didn't say anything against it. In fact, he didn't say anything against anything. He expressed what he cared about; and he let the rest go. He laughed with pleasure when I caught the puffball. A man shows what he values by what he laughs at.

He never asked for the mushroom back so I wound up holding the thing, and rolling it from hand to hand, and sometimes trying to balance it on one finger. We talked standing for awhile; we talked sitting on some boulders awhile, we lay down on the moss awhile. And he seemed to be talking from the same place. I mean as if he was the same person, not a crowd like most people: one moment interested, the next not, one moment cordial, the next not, one moment with you, the next not — a surging crowd of restless urges, all wanting to go in different directions. But he was one person.

As the morning nodded into afternoon, he rose and asked where I was headed. Since I wasn't headed anywhere I said I was looking for a spot

I'd heard about, some moss-covered sanctuary surrounded by aspen trees with a rock in the center out of which water flowed in a melodious trickle, a mystic place. Smiling, he said he knew the place, but he wasn't going there. He said he was bound for the river.

"Do you want to go too?"

Aaron had a destination. That was his name: Aaron, I'm pretty sure. Though it might have been Arnold. He mumbled sometimes, when a bald eagle swept by, or a deer appeared. But his name hardly matters. He could have had every name in the *Name Your Baby Book* and he still would have been beyond them all. There was something nameless about him. Not that he was vague or flaky. He was very definite about everything. Like his destination. You knew he had it in mind no matter what he ran into. He had it set clearly in his mind as the captain of a sailing ship has his port in mind.

We moved unhurriedly down the ridge. And

what he said most was: "Did you see that?" Usually I hadn't. A little purple flower waving in the shade, a chipmunk blinking by a fallen log, a seagull carrying a string in its beak, a rotted-out stump that looked like a Russian chapel, an albino ant, a warm ribbon of air twisting through the cool gloom of the pines, a brassiere with most of its pink and sheen drained out of it fitted demurely around a bumpy-trunked sycamore. He saw everything. I felt like a blind man. Without him pointing out one thing and another I might have only noted there were trees and rocks. (Interestingly enough, before night fell I noticed some things he missed.)

We never got to the river that night. We built a fire. I gathered wood. He got the fire going. I don't know if he had matches. He was resourceful enough to know how to rub his thumbs together and produce a spark. And as we lolled by the fire he talked about shad and pickerel and the brackish wonder of the great river we've shackled with that most unglamorous name of "Hudson."

One of the most remarkable things about the man was that he actually listened to himself talk, choosing his words like a chemist and, simultaneously, watching their effect on me. He listened to me, too. He wasn't thinking while I was talking; rather he seemed to be thinking my thoughts with me. You say different things when somebody listens to you. Not the usual foolishness; not the usual emptiness. You can say what you mean, especially if the person listening is not judging, but just listening. There was a freedom about him; he didn't have to judge. It freed me up, too.

Not that the conversation was all sober either. We joked and laughed a lot. Even that was different. There was nothing negative in the joking. After meeting him, Aaron or Arnold or Aram, whatever his name was, I noticed how much of what passes for humor is negative and demeaning. I remember laughing because what he was saying was so true. The laughter laundered us.

There was no moon that night, and the stars paraded in their slow, stately way. We watched the fire. We looked up at the stars. We sat in the same silence. I think I fell asleep once or twice, just for a twinkling. At dawn, which came with a big blush in the sky, we parted without a word, he one way and I another, without disturbing the delicate silence of the hour.

I've never seen him again, though I seem to catch pieces of him sometimes, in a crowd, on the street, in a passing car. To have come across such a man is enough, I suppose. No name, no address.

To have found such a man — a whole, integrated person, who has no contradictions, no negativity in his mind or heart, who knows what he is about, who's free, who can make a choice, and lives truly, truthfully — is a great good fortune.

Friends, I put him forward as the best man in the Hudson Valley.

And one more thing: since there is one of him

around there may well be others, here or on the way. Who knows? Watch for them. That's what I'm doing.

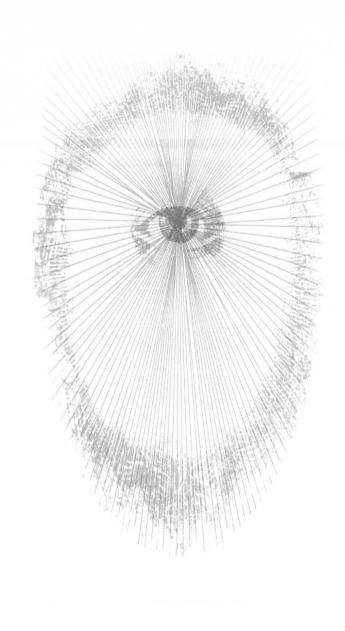

Literature Deficiency Disorder

Back then, way back when I was a skinny kid with sideburns embarking on what the catalogs and guidance counselors heralded as a "college career" (career and careen being too close in spelling for me not to suspect some diabolic connection) my father, that forthright, practical man, asked me what I was going to do there.

"There" was Brooklyn College, even then sprawling in mediocre splendor under the Flatbush sun. So I snapped back at him, for he had never finished elementary school, that I was going to study literature — English and American. Predictably, he asked me what use I could put it to. I countered that it was the only subject that interested me, and besides, I might become a writer, and if worse came to worse, I could always teach it.

Worse did come to worse, as it frequently does, and I taught literature, English and American, in high schools and colleges and universities, in the city and in the sticks, and in the process learned few were interested in "our literary heritage" and even fewer found value in it. I could stir my students and stimulate them, but they were more interested in me and my teaching style than in the material.

Now matters are at their worst: I move through my days unable to refer to writers and literary works that would enrich, expand and illuminate the scope of the conversation. If there's time and someone shows the least interest, I'll explain my reference or quote a piece of some poem or the plot of a tale. But it's like explaining the punchline of a joke to a willing but dead horse.

The literature of England and America constitutes the richest stream in all of world literature.

Think of it — Chaucer, Milton, Marlowe, Shakespeare, Donne, Herbert, Sheridan, Pope, Blake, Burns, Keats, Coleridge, Tennyson, Browning, Hopkins, Dylan Thomas, Dickens, Eliot, Pound, Hemingway, Faulkner, Whitman, Crane, Dickinson, Thoreau — work of such surpassing quality that it has influenced other literary traditions and people who speak other languages value their work even in wooden translations.

But a tradition, if it's to be a *living* tradition, has to be carried. Educational institutions, on which we benightedly rely, pass on the corpse of literature — in fact the academics refer to a writer's body of work as a *corpus*. They cannot be expected to carry the living literature of a people. The people themselves must carry the tradition in their hearts. When I was in Persia it surprised me that even the peasants valued their great lights — Rumi, Hafiz, Attar — and could quote them like a fountain, and speak their words with pride and reverence. They value what their writers brought forth into language. They recognize their treasure and pass it on to their children.

As near as I can tell we're too absorbed in the grind of life, too hypnotized by the tap dance of technology, too brainwashed by Hollywood and the media-minions to value anything other than the big, the strong, the loud and the crude. The values of literature have to do with wisdom and beauty, the refinement of being, the purifying of emotion and the cultivation of understanding in a complex and naughty world. They matter.

So, in the interest of people, and of the literature I've spent a lifetime studying, and of my father who wanted me to do something useful, I recently conducted an experiment with some students I work with. I resurrected a little play I'd written thirty years ago concerning a dramatic moment in the life of John Donne, the English metaphysical poet (most remembered nowadays for a passage in one of his Devotions that begins "No man is an Island...") who was a rake in his youth, entered the church and took to meditating on life and mortality in a coffin. Well, one day a lovely lady out of his past comes to interrupt his meditations. The play goes on from there. But to appreciate this little drama one really does have to know a bit about his life and to have a connection to his writings. So over a weekend we studied some of the prose and poems of John Donne, memorizing them and reciting them together. And the play came alive. More importantly, the works of John Donne came alive for them.

Touched by Donne's eloquence, creative turns of mind, unusual imagery and deep feeling, a lawyer in the group was heard to cry out to the heavens: "I love John Donne!" In that moment the tradition of English literature came alive in a man's heart.

"And that has made all the difference."

For those of you who have read this far, here's a poem for you, my gift to you, and to the literature.

INSIGHT IS BETTER THAN ICE CREAM

A Hopeful Promise

*Here's what I would do
if I had the opportunity:
I'd open my mouth and hope
that out would come
a flock of birds
each with a note
in its beak
that all together
in the bellowing wind
made music of a sort
to lift up dead men,
gently, of course,
from their graves.*

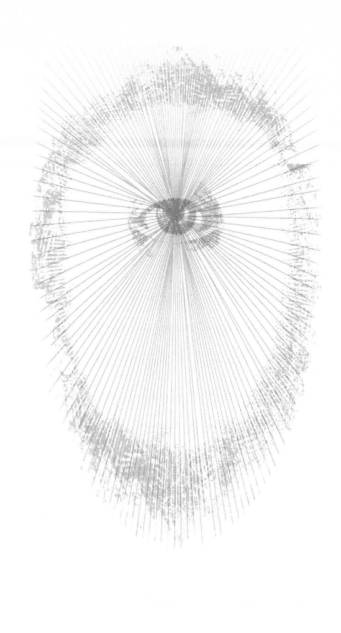

PITY THE CHILDREN
AN OPEN LETTER TO WHOMEVER
CARES FOR THE YOUNG

Dear Whomever:

I would have written this letter to God if I thought He would impose His Enlightenment upon the willfully ignorant. I write it to you in the hope that your ears are not so full of wax that you can't hear. And if you can hear, perhaps you can summon the fire that compels action. Who else can I turn to?

Because the children can't say it themselves; because they fall in with whatever parade happens to be passing; because they'll make the best of the worst bargain — I've undertaken to speak on their behalf. After all, what is my mouth for if not for the downtrodden, the abused, misused, ignored, deprived, malnourished, misguided, mutilated and the helpless? So I'll aim at one target, and only one, leaving the others for another day.

It's about this matter of literacy. Somewhere, sometime, some ignoramus got it into his or her head that we should foist the printed word onto children as soon as we can. As is the way of the world, with a little fanfare and a few interviews, this notion became widespread, respectable, all the rage. Now kindergarten ("the children's garden") — no, that's not soon enough — Pre-K, Pre-Pre-K, Nursery! Why, if these idiots have their way, they'll find means to press inky characters onto the eyeballs of babes in cradles!

And for what, I ask you? So kids will turn out as stupid, as one-sided, as unbalanced, as victim-ized by "ideas" as the daydreamers who came up with the whole scheme? That would be the hon-est answer. In the absence of honesty they'll give us mutterings about the modern world, progress, being college-bound (i.e. hand and foot), good citizenship, intelligence and God help us, literacy.

When a child learns is everything. The body has a lot of developing to do, and it must learn to move in multifarious ways; the emotional life has to stretch; the social sense, common sense, the sense of humor, as well as the physical senses (the seven of them) — all need to grow. The new, fresh being needs time and space to develop these and many other capacities before being stamped with the stultifying rigidity of the written word. If reading and 'riting strike too soon, the child's other capacities are stunted. And if you need proof of early literacy's stunting power, take a look at today's crop of kids.

Rudolf Steiner, who knew a thing or two, is perceived as a fuddy-duddy nowadays, and, admittedly he does have a touch of it, and the system of education he inspired has an old-fashioned Teutonic smell to it, but when it comes to the detrimental effects of teaching reading and 'riting too early, he was right on the money.

As if this wasn't bad enough, look at what these neglected and victimized children are given to apply their new-found skill to: cereal boxes, labels, signs, magazines, billboards, newspapers, matchbook covers, menus, computer manuals and a tumbling, stupendous smorgasbord of tripe relentlessly provided by young people's publishers who will, in their turn, soon be replaced by old people's publishers. Thus having become literate, children can and will read all the useless, eye wearying, vulgar, empty, carcinogenic junk we provide for them.

The mark of literacy is not that you *can* read but that you know *what* to read. Alas, in this the children have no guidance. For here we leave litter-a-see in all its trashy variety and bring in the nearly extinct bird of literature.

My dear Whomever, I am not so naïve as to believe the world will suddenly wake up and our so-called educational system will cease to mutilate the essence of our children. So we must do what we can do to make it up to them. One way we can do it is to let them have literature. I mean poems and plays and tales and novels of quality. Regardless of the nutrient-free pap they're getting in the school, we must supply what's needed at home. These children need the food of meaning. They need to know of the beautiful. They need to hear of values above the sitcom level. They need to develop a rich emotional life. They need to know that there have been men and women who have thought high thoughts and done high deeds. They need to know and experience, through direct contact, that there is a higher life possible even in the midst of the fast accumulating dungheap of the modern world. Literature can supply this.

What to read? What's worth reading? Ah, that shall have to wait for another time and another letter. Suffice it to say that there is an abundance for those who seek. And if you need something, any old something, here's something. A fragment about a seagull by a writer named Coleridge. He's the fellow who wrote of Kubla Khan and albatrosses. And this is merely an obscure morsel in a cornucopia of great work:

Fragment
Seaward, white gleaming thro' the busy scud
With arching Wings, the sea-mew o'er my head
Posts on, as bent on speed, now passaging
Edges the stiffer Breeze, now, yielding, drifts,
Now floats upon the air, and sends from far
A wildly wailing Note.

That's all. Five and a half lines. But it makes it worth knowing how to read. And there's much more where that came from. Much more.

Pity the Children.

Yours in truth,

Frank

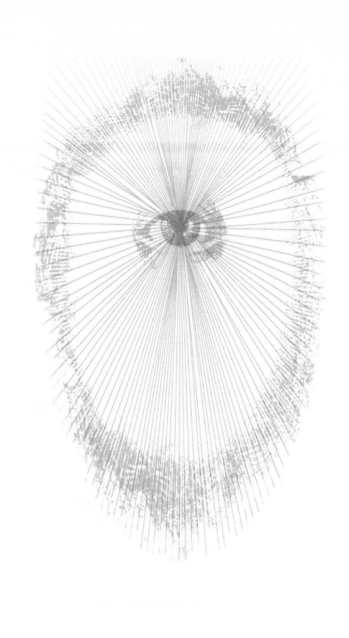

Who Will Lead Me Out of Darkness

The Letter

Dear Satan,

This is my very first personal letter to you, so I find myself at a loss to know exactly how to address you properly: "Your Highness?...Your Lowness?...Your Majesty?...Your Abyssal Majesty?...Your Royal, Revered Lord of the Dark?" Do you have a preference? Would you consider being called just "Friend?" Would you find that excessively, insultingly familiar? Have I crossed over the line of good taste? One never knows how things come to pop into one's head. (I mean that we, humans, never know. You, of course, must surely know.) "Friend" is a fine term and I use it advisedly, with some confidence in its appropriateness. (Friend, with a capital F, to be sure.) Like any true friend (I didn't mean to use that word "true;" pardon me) you have been beside me, often behind, and always backing me up. I might even say, *faithfully* backing me up. I don't mean to imply there was any virtue in it, of course. It's just that I've always felt you and your constant presence like a furry shadow in a dark alleyway.

Only once did you actually reveal yourself to me. I must admit I had not been looking for you, though I had heard, and did occasionally realize, that you were posing as a priest or a minister or doctor or nurse or psychiatrist or social worker or artist or teacher or even sometimes a politician — although I must say, in the latter case, the disguise seemed rather transparent. But to see you in all your glory was reserved for one very special time. Perhaps you remember?

It was long, long ago, when I was just a pup. Eight or nine, as I remember. (I should have marked it on the calendar. I keep on neglecting to do that. My whole life has nearly gone by and I don't have an accurate chronology of when the important things happened. I suppose that's because nothing seemed so historically important at the time it was happening.) Yes, I was eight or nine years old at the time. And I was sick. How I loved being sick when I was a boy! I was sick and I was in bed.

Then you appeared at the foot of my bed. What a moment! Surely you remember. Ah, I'm sure you do. You're not one for forgetting. You never forget. That's one of the most reassuring facts about you. We, humans, may forget; we may even forget ourselves, but you never forget us, not even for a moment. (That must indicate that we are worth something, wouldn't you say? To put it philosophically, that we have "inherent value." Eh?)

I'm sorry, I don't want to put words in your mouth, my Friend. It's just that you do have a re-markable constancy and dependability about you. And as friends, shouldn't we be able to be open and truthful? I can be truthful with you. For example: all my sicknesses have been attempts to dodge things. (I was a real Brooklyn dodger. Yuk, yuk.) And when I was a kid the only thing worth dodging was school. (School! Now there's a word to conjure with. I'll get to that soon enough.) So sometimes I lied. Which I'm sure you appreciated. And sometimes I was sort of sick and by working at it was able to make myself more so. And other times, all too infrequently, I was honest-to-God sick.

The time I'm telling you about, I was really sick. I had a raging fever. In fact, now that I'm thinking about it, it must have been scarlet fever. (It ran like a rash through the student body in those days.) The shades were down; my mother was running in and out, bringing me water, taking my temperature, cooling my brow with cold cloths, and spreading alcohol over my whole body to bring down the flames.

Then you appeared. Remember? My mother had just left the room. I was alone in a brownish-pink haze. My eyes were closed, and my brain was spinning like a dervish. "Frankie..." I thought sure I heard a voice. It was a soft voice, like the rustling of silk. I didn't want to open my eyes because I'd been told the light could make me blind. Also, I thought maybe my Uncle Vito might have sneaked in and was fooling around. I wasn't going to be made a fool of. After all, I was really sick. Then the voice rustled again: "Frankie, my boy."

"Go 'way," I said.

"It's me," you said.

The way you said, "It's me," made me open my eyes. You said it so familiarly.

There you were — smiling and clean shaven and it seemed to me in my feverish state that you had steam coming off you. My eyes felt like they had pieces of grit floating in them; I could barely keep them open. I remember moaning; that was more for sympathy than a reaction toward you.

You seemed extremely likable to me. Yet I couldn't help wondering how you had gotten into the room.

You said something about how good it was to see an old pal. That was the word you used, "pal." I remember it because I thought about the PAL (Police Athletic League) and that maybe you were connected to the cops. I didn't like cops and I didn't like the PAL. I began feeling nervous. And then you laughed, and I began to be even more nervous. Finally, I asked you what the hell you wanted. I meant no offense. That's just how it came out. Then you touched my toes, and that was it. I screamed for Mom.

She came crashing in like a locomotive.

"What's the matter?"

"The devil's here," I screamed, scrinching my eyes closed. "He's in the room."

"You're delirious. Oh my God. Oh, my poor boy. You're going to give me a heart attack."

(My recollection is that I was always bringing

my mother to the brink of a heart attack.)

I opened my eyes a little.

"He was right there, by the bed. He touched my toes."

My mother said something in Italian and she made the sign of the cross. And that was it. Once she made the sign of the cross (and Mom rarely made the sign of the cross) it was all over. I wasn't even sure myself if it had actually happened. That made it worse in a way, because it showed me the power of my own imagination. Especially when it was out of my control. Then Mom held me awhile and murmured things about imagining and delirium and pretty soon I was asleep.

Now, my Friend, now that I have your eye, so to speak, there are a few things I have always wondered about:

> 1. Why did you make such a hasty exit when I called for my mother?
>
> 2. Was it merely accidental that you decided to go just then?

3. Did you have other pressing business?

4. Had you had previous encounters with my mother?

I don't mean to pry. And I really don't expect you to tell me the truth one way or another. Frankly speaking, I just wanted to get it out there.

But to get to the real purpose of this letter, my dear Friend:

Over the last half century or so since you visited that little boy burning in his scarlet fever, I have come to admire you with an admiration close to adoration. Not for you personally, for I hardly know you, but for your methods and the results they achieve. You are able, with such consummate mastery, to undo our best efforts, to turn things into their opposite, to create new hydra-headed problems with each solution we reach, to cause even the most pure-minded and best-intentioned among us to lose our way, see things upside down, and instead of moving further and further towards the light, head deeper into the darkness.

Who Will Lead Me Out of Darkness...

Please don't think that I am going through all this trouble to flatter you. Far be it from me to flatter you or anyone. I merely want to let the truth be spoken. Not to speak of the fact that anyone who knows anything knows that you are far beyond the reach of flattery, or falsity of any kind. After all, you are the Master of it. I simply want to give you your due. And you do what you do very, very well.

What's more, I have no personal agenda in all this. I don't want any personal favors. I don't want any special treatment. I don't want you to ease up on me, either. I like things just the way they are. I like the charge you bring into things. I like the stakes, and I like the challenge.

But what am I writing to you for, you may ask, and I'm sure you are? I have a question. It's about something that happened a while ago, and since the damage has been done I don't think it will make any difference one way or the other to give me an answer to my question. All right? My question is: How did you do it? It's like asking a magician to tell how he did his trick, I know, except in this case, since you have so many tricks, all ever-new, in fact a new one for each occasion, to answer my question is to divulge nothing at all. What do you say, my Friend? Yes?

The question is attached to an event. So I have to give you some background. To refresh your memory. This is the story:

Years ago in the wonderful once-upon-a-time when I had all my hair there was a school. You guessed it: this is about EDUCATION. It was a very well-moneyed school, well-endowed you might say, a high school, and fittingly, it was set high upon a hill. The light from that school could be seen for miles, even from the other side of the river. For over a century it carried on its well-publicized tradition. And each autumn like gnat-swarms, "young-a-dolts" from many an odd corner of the world — Japan, Mexico, Italy, even Flatbush — converged onto that mountaintop.

Who Will Lead Me Out of Darkness...

There, high on the hill, these young men and women lodged and boarded, and despite the manifest inconvenience and continuous intrusion upon their plans and preferences, they were required to attend classes. Alas, the classes were not always well-attended, were often noisy and produced little in the way of scholarly result. To make matters worse, the teachers were treated with such consistent and creative disrespect it bordered on artistry. Each entering freshman class was regaled with high tales of the tradition of teacher maltreatment, the peak of which had been reached but a mere two years before I joined the so-called faculty. An educated man, a poet, an English teacher had been bound hand-and-foot to a lavatory seat, had suffered the night and had only been found and released the next morning. Ah, they took pride in the telling of the tale, and there was much jocularity all around when they did. This was only part of the general mayhem and the long tradition of hooliganism that prevailed upon the hill.

Insight is Better Than Ice Cream

And so, amidst beautifully manicured grounds and fine works of architecture, "education" went on year after year. But, as you may know, things do not and cannot remain bad for long; they must (by law) go from bad to worse. And so they did.

Eventually, the faculty, a motley crew dredged from the four corners also, resolved to have a meeting. They were typical of most faculties in that they were seized by the double delusion that they knew something and could do something. In this case they believed they could do something about the "educational state of affairs." At a much-trumpeted meeting, in an atmosphere of hopeful hullabaloo, the faculty unanimously resolved to face the issue squarely. Clearly, something needed to be done. And what was done was this: A series of serious meetings were held analyzing what went wrong with education and what was needed to make it right. Out of these many meetings was to come a book, a great book, a definitive book on the proper education of young adults in the 20th Century!

188

(I'm sure you remember all this. You must have found it very amusing.)

Much was pronounced; much was proclaimed. And much was written down during the interminable course of these many meetings. But there was one particular thing that occurred that I wish to point out to you. One teacher there was, a relatively new member of the faculty, who nursed some dark doubts about the utility of the whole affair, but who, overcoming his usual reluctance, vowed to make a "contribution." The young man, and he was young at the time, suggested, in a humble voice, that since no learning could take place without attention — in any school — students should be taught to pay attention. He could have gone on and pointed out that the result of inattention is boredom and that discipline would take care of itself when the students, as the consequence of using their attention, became interested and motivated, but he feared overstating his case and let it go at that.

Insight is Better Than Ice Cream

Of course, once he had spoken the faculty nodded, unanimously. (I'm sure you recall this, sir.)

At the end of the year the faculty committee produced a very beautiful book. The book was blue and bound and gold-edged. Copies went to each member of the faculty, each administrator, every last one of the trustees, even to the parents of the young adults whose wayward behavior had inspired the tome. Two copies went to the school library and copies were dispatched to the Library of Congress. It was a magnificent achievement.

Everything was included in that beautiful book. Every word ever spoken by members of the deliberating faculty was printed there. Every word, every jot and tittle, except that one little sentence about the importance of attention in the educational process.

Alas and well-a-day.

I suppose it could have been predicted. I couldn't have, though. I thought it would get in.

After all, what's the harm in a little sentence about paying attention? No one was going to read the book anyway.

So, what I want to know, Mr. Satan, my Friend, is how in heaven's name did you do it? How could so many seemingly intelligent people dismiss the importance of attention? Did they really see no value in it? Did you place a veil over their eyes? You had to have done something. Now, tell me, won't you? It was you, wasn't it? Was it an oversight? Or was it the work of the printer's devil? Tell me, won't you?

Hoping to hear from you, I am and remain

Frankly yours,

Frank

P.S. I know this story seems like a parable, but you and I know it really happened.

THE REPLY

Dearest F —

Hot stuff. I remember it well. Hopeless nincompoops. Great fun, though. How'd I dood it? Simple. I help them to see everything upside down and backwards and then I whisper to them about how high their I.Q.s are. As long as they think they know something they won't listen to anything, no matter how true it is.

Am enclosing for your diabolical amusement the twelve most unquestioned assumptions about EDUCATION. I put them upside down because that's how these asses see things. Yuk,yuk.

Oh, by the way, Frankie Boy, to avoid any complications, implications, supplications or explications, burn this epistle once you've read it. You heard me, burn it! It's just between you and me. Right, buddy?

Your Eternal Friend,
His Abyssal Majesty (I like that.)

P.S.

Your mother didn't scare me one bit!

1. That we do not have to learn to pay
   attention in order to learn.
2. That people prefer the light to the darkness.
3. That bureaucrats can regulate the art
   of teaching.
4. That all that needs to be educated
   is the head.
5. That so-called educational institutions can
   distinguish between the relevant
   and the irrelevant.
6. That the storing-up of irrelevant facts
   adds up to education.
7. That a faculty that has lost its faculties has
   the faculty to teach.
8. That you can teach someone who doesn't
   want to learn.
9. That research can replace search.
10. That education has to do with books.
11. That education takes place in a classroom.
12. That the ignorant can communicate
    knowledge to the ignorant.

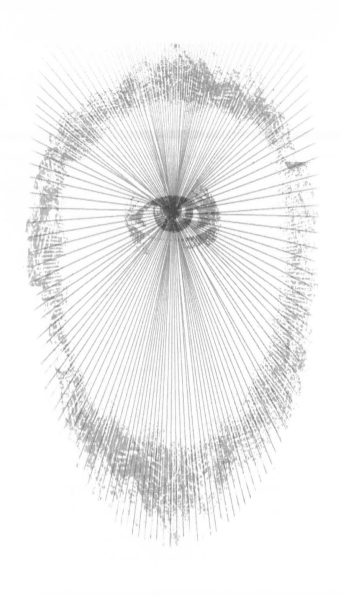

Thank You, My Dear Death

She seized my arm and asked "Frank, are we dead yet?"

It was three o'clock of a black still night. I had been reading. Her question startled me. When I saw she was still asleep I was amused, and with dubious conviction, I assured her that we were not there yet. "Oh," she said as she sank back onto her pillow. Then she murmured "Thanks."

I looked at her a while, this woman I call my wife. She went back to her dreaming. She asked that question with the chilling matter-of-factness that voices breaking from dreams have. This must have come out of that recurring death dream she has had as long as I've known her.

INSIGHT IS BETTER THAN ICE CREAM

At least she thinks about it, I thought, at least she dreams about it. It beats trying to ignore it.

I've never been able to ignore it myself. Ever since I heard my parents and my uncle talking about it in the kitchen the summer that I was ten. I lay there in bed listening till the realization crushed me. Everybody was going to die. I turned my face to the wall and wept till I fell asleep. It was a very long time before sleep came, though.

Death has never been far away. The closest call came when I was rushed to the hospital at the age of 12. I had bulbar polio and I was supposed to die that night. Of course I didn't know that at the time. I just knew I was seeing double, I had a pain in my side like a knife, and I retched up anything that went to my stomach.

Over the years I've tried different ways of relating to death. In my teens I tried running from it. The old *Appointment in Samarra* story, where a man tries to evade death by running to the very town where Death is going to meet him, put an end to that idea.

I turned to wooing it in my twenties, and wrote a file-full of embarrassing poems on death. I took to arm-wrestling it in my thirties, laughed it to scorn in my forties, defied it in my fifties and now, from my over-the-hill position at 62, I almost have a mind to welcome it.

I have a sense that I have made a circle and returned to a view of Death that I had when I was very young and would play-act elaborate, triumphant ways of dying. I had a relish for it, and always got up laughing. My friends and I were always at war or having showdowns with swords or guns or anything we could vaguely turn into a gun. We practiced dying on the streets of Brooklyn.

Now that I think of it, I had a similar feeling when I played Mercutio. As I stumbled, gasping, after Tybalt's villainous sword-thrust under Romeo's arm and into my side, I joked. When asked how my wound was I replied as only a Veronese wiseguy would:

Insight is Better Than Ice Cream

" 'Tis not so deep as a well nor so wide as a church door but 'tis enough, twill serve..."

Alas, when Mercutio dies, he takes the life of the play with him.

What obscures the issue and makes the relationship to Death so difficult to get right is the bad press Death has gotten. The dark, hooded figure, skeleton-faced, holding his ominous, well-whetted scythe. O'Neill had a far more appealing symbol. He has Yank on his deathbed on the S.S. Glencairn, his broken body wracked with pain, raise himself up and describe the beautiful lady in black he sees beckoning at the door. Perhaps Death's not as dreadful as we've been led to believe.

The beauty part of it all is that with Death, whether Miz or Mister, there are no deals, no privileged characters, no exceptions. Everybody must meet it. Alexander, Ghengis Khan, Buddha, Jesus, Faustus, Steiner, Gurdjieff, Sherlock Holmes, James Dean. All, all have been taken by the hand

and led over the threshold. Even you and I — we who secretly believe it won't happen to us — even you and I must keep our appointment.

After all, why not you and me? We who have measured out our lives in coffee spoons; we who have had our noses wiped, our health insured, our portfolios managed; who've never contributed one iota's-worth of value to the world; why should we be exceptions?

Death breaks our dream of life with the finality of a spoon cracking an eggshell. All our cleverness, all our laughter, all our superiority over others, all our schemes, our glories, our triumphs come to an abrupt end.

This is all pathetically obvious, for anyone who wants to see it. These are just the facts. But what I want to know is: Why are we alive? And what is the point of this shadow of Death? And what comes after? This is what I've always wanted to know.

So I asked people if they knew what life is

about, what Death is and what comes after Death. All they could come up with was more and more hooey. Yes, they gave me their opinions. And what they like to believe. I saw they didn't know what life was; they seemed lifeless themselves. I realized they had no way of knowing the what or the why of Death; they were hoping and praying and pretending it didn't exist. And as to what comes after: the religious said there was an afterlife and the non-religious said there was none. Both camps made the same muffled and hollow sound peculiar to people when they're talking through their hats.

Then, having despaired of squeezing anything out of my contemporaries, I turned to books. I read what the dead said when they were living. I read the books of wise men, and I came across nothing but well-expressed opinions. They said exactly what people would say when they really don't know.

Where, then, can one go to know?

Is it possible to know?

Do we have to depend upon someone coming back from the dead to tell us?

Could we and would we trust them, anyway?

Then I turned to life itself. And I found there in life, in the living, the answer to all my questions. Which is, as it turned out, but one question.

What threw me off initially was the assumption that being alive had to do with breathing and biology. This so-called life is merely existence, an existence that gives us the opportunity to come to life. Life, the real thing, is in us — we have to find it, we have to wake up to it, we have to immerse ourselves in it. The more pertinent middle-of-the-night question is:

"Are we alive yet, Frank?"

When we catch fire and feel life burning in us, then we can see why Mr. Death or the Dark Lady is lurking in the wings. He or She is there to spur us on to more and more intense life by reminding us that we have but little time, there's no putting it off, *now* we must live! Death, when seen rightly, is a friend. By keeping a constant awareness of Death we can drink deep of the precious waters of life.

Once we've come to life and are one with it we belong to that ever-bubbling fountain that streams everlastingly. For those who have come to that life there is no stoppage, nor is there an "afterlife." There is only a continuing life. The nature of life is to go on and on.

Where does that leave Death, you may say, poor, pallid shadow? He has one last service to perform for us, and that is to usher us over the threshold into a large, well-lit room where all's exquisite, where all's gorgeous, where all's abundant. This is the place where Life flourishes, expands and comes to ever-increasing fullness. This is where those who love life go. This is where the Great Ones have gone and where they beckon us to come. This is the place the great Zarathushtra called "The House of Song."

Sunnyside   *New Paltz, NY*

An Invitation…

If you have found any of these tales stimulating, and you'd like to know more, about the Work I teach or how it might relate to your life, I invite you to contact me at Discovery Institute.

A group of us have been working together for some time now, putting this Work into practice, making it real in our lives.

You can reach us at the address below.

Fare well in all your endeavors.

Discovery Institute
64 Plains Road
New Paltz, NY 12561
914 255-5548
discover@bestweb.net

Other Works
by Frank Crocitto

Hooray for Love
A Child's Christmas in Brooklyn
Rumi Is Alive

Hooray for Love is also available in audio format